PRAISE FOR M

"A literar

—*The Daily Telegraph*

"Absolutely brilliant."

—*The Daily Mail*

"Atticus Priest will be the star of many future novels."

—*Richard Madeley*

"Nerve-shreddingly tense. Utterly addictive."

— *MJ Arlidge*

"Dawson writes the kind of thrillers I love. Non-stop, grab-you-by-the-throat tales of doing the right thing no matter the odds. Simply excellent."

—*Brett Battles*

"A terrific, fast-paced read. Mark Dawson knows how to tell a great story."

—*Scott Mariani*

"Mark Dawson has all the skills. A great thriller writer on the top of his game."

—*Steve Cavanagh*

MORE THAN 18,000 FIVE STAR AMAZON REVIEWS

"Fast paced and a wonderful read."

"Brilliantly written - Dawson's best yet."

"Totally hooked now."

"Unbelievable!"

"Made me fall in love with reading again."

"Cannot get enough of these books."

"Wow - what a read."

"Brilliant, brilliant, brilliant!"

MARK DAWSON

THE CASEBOOK OF ATTICUS PRIEST

First published in 2025 by Unputdownable Limited

A CIP catalogue of record for this book is available from the British Library.

Paperback ISBN: 978-1-0687754-5-1

Typeset by Riverside Publishing Solutions Ltd (UK)
Printed and bound by CPI Group (UK), Ltd., Croydon, CR0 4YY.

FSC
www.fsc.org
MIX
Paper | Supporting responsible forestry
FSC® C013604

ALSO BY MARK DAWSON

In The Atticus Priest Series

The House in the Woods
A Place to Bury Strangers
The Red Room
All the Devils are Here
The Inheritance

In The John Milton Series

The Cleaner
Saint Death
The Driver
Ghosts
The Sword of God
Salvation Row
Headhunters
The Ninth Step
The Jungle
Blackout
The Alamo
Redeemer
Sleepers
Twelve Days
Bright Lights
The Man Who Never Was
Killa City
Ronin
Never Let Me Down Again
Bulletproof
Uppercut
Bloodlands
Vultures
The Hanging Tree
Clearwater

In The Beatrix Rose Series

In Cold Blood
Blood Moon Rising
Blood and Roses
The Dragon and the Ghost
Tempest
Phoenix

In The Isabella Rose Series

The Angel
The Asset
The Agent
The Assassin
The Avenger
Pretty Face

In The Charlie Cooper Series

Sandstorm
The Chameleon
Blood Brothers
Dead of Winter
Code Blue
North Star
Collateral
Leverage
Burnout
Exposure
Heatwave

THE MYSTERY OF THE MISSING PAGES

1

I received Atticus's summons at a little after ten o'clock in the evening on Christmas Eve. It wasn't the first time he'd called me at a late hour—that honour went to a call at one in the morning after he'd been locked out of his flat—but this message, as terse as always, had an urgency about it that I couldn't ignore:

Stockbridge, Lydia Marchant's house. ASAP!

I'd only been working for Atticus for a few months, and even in that short time, I'd learned two things: first, that his notion of "urgent" was wildly elastic, and second, that his eccentricity wasn't limited to his approach to cases. The fact that he didn't even acknowledge that it was Christmas Eve, and that I might be busy (even though I wasn't), would turn out to be a standard reflection of the way he was. I'd already noticed that he often forgot things that might be important to others and had started to suspect he might be on the spectrum. There would be plenty of other examples over the course of the next few months that would confirm my admittedly amateur diagnosis.

Our introduction hadn't been auspicious: I'd been hired by a woman to investigate her husband, and Atticus had been hired by the husband to investigate her. We'd both been press-ganged into representing opposite sides of what was already a spectacularly bitter matrimonial dispute.

Atticus eventually contacted me to offer me a job. I'd only recently begun my career as an investigator, and the chance to learn from someone as brilliant as him seemed almost too good to be true. It turned out that he was struggling to keep up with demand; his name had gained a certain notoriety, and he'd decided to expand. Winchester was his chosen outpost, a location he deemed suitably affluent, manageable in size, and, in his words, "civilised enough without being entirely smug." It was one of his more sensible decisions, though I'd already learned to temper my expectations where Atticus and sensibility were concerned. I lived in Winchester and had useful connections there, and so it was that we agreed on terms, and I started to look for an office on the High Street.

Lydia Marchant's name rang no bells, but a quick Google search before I set off revealed a titan of the literary world. She was the agent of agents, the king and queen maker of bestsellers, a woman who could pluck a debut author from obscurity and turn them into a household name. Her annual Christmas party was legendary, though reserved for her most cherished clients. The idea of Atticus attending such a soirée was almost laughable; he barely tolerated pleasantries, let alone grand affairs.

It sounded intriguing and, six months later, as I look back on my notes of what happened that night it seems obvious that it be the first case I write up for the as-yet undefined project that I've been considering. Atticus is an extraordinary investigator, and I'm pretty sure there'll be an audience for a telling of the tales we have encountered together. I am aware, of course, of the obvious antecedent and, if that makes me Watson to his Holmes, then so be it. I'm not sure *how* I will publish the stories yet; Conan Doyle had *The Strand* magazine to publish his, and I might look to Substack or Medium or perhaps self-publish them and see if they take off.

The Casebook of Atticus Priest has a ring to it.

* * *

It took twenty-five minutes to drive from Winchester to Stockbridge and, by the time I pulled into the gravel drive of Lydia's estate, frost had settled thickly over the grounds. It crunched beneath my feet as I stepped out of the car. The house itself was a vision of Georgian splendour, its symmetrical façade featuring sash windows adorned with festive wreaths. Lights picked out the gravel path and the intricate shapes of topiary that could have been from one of the costumed dramas with which the BBC was carpet bombing the Christmas schedule.

I found Atticus in the back garden, standing beneath a yew tree with his coat collar turned up against the chill. There was an intensity in his posture, hands clasped behind his back, his breath curling in the icy air. The scent of something sweet and herbal told me he was smoking one of his 'special' cigarettes.

"Jeremy," he greeted without turning.

"Jez," I reminded him for what must've been the twentieth time since I had started working for him. "Only my mother calls me Jeremy."

"Jez," he amended, glancing over with a faint smile. "Thanks for coming."

"Not a problem," I replied, blowing into my hands to keep warm. "Though I'd appreciate knowing why I'm standing in a frozen garden at this hour."

"We'll get to that," he said, holding up the joint. "Want a toke?"

"I'll pass," I said.

"It's good."

"Not my thing. What's going on?"

He gestured to the stone bench nearby. "Sit. Explaining it to you will help me organise my thoughts."

"Can't we do this inside, where it's warm?"

"Not an option," he said. "Can't risk anyone overhearing."

"Who?"

"Them—the guests. You'll see. There's been a bit of a scandal."

Reluctantly, I settled on the bench, the cold biting through my jeans.

Atticus began pacing, his hands tucked behind his back. "You've heard of Lydia Marchant?"

"Looked her up. Big deal in publishing."

"She is," he said. "And she invited me here tonight."

"Why?"

"She's my agent," he said with a trace of irony. "She thinks my *Notes on Deductive Reasoning* could fetch a decent advance."

I raised an eyebrow. "Rubbing shoulders with literary royalty now?"

"Something like that," he said. "Though it turns out that me being here might be more useful than Lydia thought."

He went on to describe the party: a weekend gathering of literary heavyweights and rising stars, each nursing egos as large as their advances. Lydia, Atticus explained, revelled in curating an occasion that would remind them of the depth of her little black book and the good sense of allowing her to continue taking her fifteen percent.

Atticus explained how the evening had been building towards a climactic moment: the unveiling of the author Eleanor Pierce's long-awaited sequel to *Solstice in September*. Even I'd heard of the book; it had been a literary phenomenon, adapted into an Oscar-winning film. The sequel was something of a myth, whispered about for years but never confirmed—until tonight.

"Eleanor excused herself to retrieve the manuscript from Lydia's study," Atticus said. "But when she returned, she didn't have it."

"What happened?"

"She said it was missing," he said simply.

"No copy?"

"She doesn't keep one. Thinks it's bad luck. Simone Bradley accused her of staging a publicity stunt; Tom Grayson said it was the most interesting thing Eleanor had done in years. Lydia was mortified, insisted the safe was secure and that theft was impossible. That's when she asked me to intervene."

"What about the safe?" I asked. "Did you check it?"

"Of course," he said. "No signs of forced entry. And Lydia swears only she and Eleanor knew the combination."

"And the thief?"

"Still here," he said. "The cameras outside show no movement. Whoever took it is one of the guests—or the staff."

I leaned back, letting the information settle. "So you've got a locked-room mystery, a house full of suspects, and a stolen manuscript—"

"—worth millions," he finished, checking his watch. "And now that you're here, we can begin."

2

I followed Atticus through the grand hallway of Lydia Marchant's house and towards the study. It was warm, with old cast iron radiators pumping out heat and a fire roaring in a large fireplace. The din of chatter and clinking glasses drifted from the sitting room, where the guests had evidently gathered, subdued but far from silent. Tinsel had been draped over the frames of the portraits hanging from the wall and a clump of mistletoe was suspended from the ceiling above the fireplace. The gentle strains of a piano rendition of 'Silent Night' were playing from somewhere. Despite the festive air, there was a palpable sense of tension.

A woman was waiting for us in the hallway, standing beneath a garland of ivy and gold ribbon. She was tall, perhaps five foot nine, with a willowy frame and a grace that suggested she was used to commanding attention. Her sleek blonde hair was impeccably styled in a sharp bob that skimmed her jawline, and her makeup was flawless; subtle but enough to highlight high cheekbones and almond-shaped eyes. She was dressed in a glamorous evening gown of deep emerald-green silk, the fabric shimmering softly in the light as it hugged her figure and flared slightly at the hem. A pair of gold stiletto heels added an extra level of hauteur to her already statuesque presence. Around her neck hung a delicate chain with a charm that looked like it might be an old family heirloom. There was tension in her shoulders and a faint tightness around her mouth. Her hands—long fingers tipped with perfectly manicured nails in a neutral shade—were held clasped together in front of her, the knuckles just slightly whitened.

"Lydia," Atticus said. "This is my colleague—Jeremy Hardwicke."

"Mr. Hardwicke," she said.

I glanced over at Atticus. "Call me Jez."

"Thank you for coming, Jez."

I took her hand briefly: her skin was soft, and I caught the faintest trace of a floral perfume. I was working on my cold reading—Atticus was teaching me the basics—and she struck me as someone used to being in control, someone who'd spent years cultivating an image of unflappability. Yet tonight, the smallest cracks were showing. Her composure had been stretched thin by the theft and, I imagined, the consequences of the manuscript going missing while in her custody. She was fighting to protect her reputation, and possibly her career.

There was an awkward silence, and I hurried to fill it. "You have a lovely house," I said gauchely.

"Thank you," she said. "although goodness knows who'll come to visit me now if we can't sort out what's happening tonight."

"I'm sure we'll be able to get to the bottom of it," Atticus said. "Shall we start?"

Lydia led us to a heavy oak door at the far end of the hall. She opened the door to reveal a room that wouldn't have looked out of place in the pages of *Tatler*. Bookshelves lined three walls, holding a tapestry of leather-bound volumes with gilded spines. A Persian rug covered the floor, its intricate patterns muted in the soft lamplight. The fourth wall was dominated by a large desk: I saw neatly stacked papers, a brass lamp, and a delicate porcelain teacup sat on a matching saucer. In the corner, a sturdy safe stood open, its door yawning like a broken jaw.

"It was in there," Atticus said to me, gesturing to the safe.

He stepped forward, crouching to inspect it. I lingered by the doorway, content to observe.

"What's the combination?" he asked.

"Two-eight-one-one. It's my daughter's birthday."

"And only you and Eleanor knew it?"

"Yes," she said. "Absolutely."

"You said Eleanor took the book out to work on it?"

"Yes," she said. "Just after lunch."

"When did she return it?"

"She said it was around half past three."

I noticed her shift slightly, the tiniest flicker of unease crossing her face. It was gone as quickly as it appeared, but Atticus had already moved on. He stood and gestured to the desk.

"Anything disturbed here?" he asked, gesturing to the papers.

"No," Lydia replied. "It's just as I left it."

"How many people have been in this room tonight?"

"Just Eleanor and me," Lydia replied, but then she faltered. "At least… I think so. The guests have been moving about freely, and Jonathan—the caretaker—has been in and out. The serving girl, too."

"But not actually in here? In this room?"

"Not that I know of, but it's not as if I keep the door locked. And it's just next to the downstairs cloakroom—it would've been possible for someone to come in if they wanted to."

Atticus nodded, moving towards the French doors at the far end of the study. He knelt, his gaze going to a faint splash of mud against the polished floor.

"These were locked earlier," Lydia said, pre-empting his question. "But it's possible someone opened them—the key was in the lock. We had the heating on. Guests were complaining it was too warm."

"Are the doors alarmed?" I asked.

"No," Lydia said. "This is Stockbridge, not the middle of London. I didn't think..." She trailed off, and for a moment, she looked genuinely distraught. "I'm so sorry. I didn't think anything like this could happen."

Atticus turned to her. "It's probably not your fault," he said.

I winced at his lack of tact.

Lydia's eyes widened. "Probably?"

"Apologies," Atticus said, his tone softening just enough to sound contrite. "That came out wrong. What I meant is that I haven't spoken to anybody yet. I'll need to do that before I can start eliminating suspects. I'll need to know their movements since they arrived."

Lydia straightened, her hands clasping together again. "I can help with that," she said.

Atticus glanced at me. "Could you take a note?"

I opened my bag and took out the notebook my girlfriend had bought for me when I told her I was leaving journalism to become a detective. The cover was headed 'List of Times I

Was Right But Nobody Listened;' Rachel thought that was hilarious. I opened the book to a fresh page, took out my pen and nodded that I was ready.

"I arrived at seven," Atticus said. "I was the last to get here. What about the others?"

"Simone and Richard Bradley arrived early," Lydia began. "Ten o'clock this morning. They spent most of the afternoon in the sitting room. Richard dominated most of the conversations, as usual."

Atticus nodded. "Go on."

"Tom Grayson must have got here half an hour later. He made himself the centre of attention, loud and charming as ever," Lydia said, though there was a distinct dryness to her words.

I put a question mark after 'charming'; it felt less like a compliment and more like a polite mistruth.

"Milo Yates?" Atticus asked, using his full name for my benefit.

"Milo," Lydia said with a soft sigh. "Poor thing. He's sweet, but I think this crowd is a bit much for him. He got here at half-eleven, but he's been in his room a lot. Bit of an introvert. Said he needed to recharge."

I jotted that down. His absence sounded like an opportunity to visit the study, perhaps unnoticed.

"Clara Wainwright?" Atticus prompted.

"Got here at eleven. Spent most of the afternoon with me." Lydia rolled her eyes. "She's relentless. Always pitching ideas, always angling. Charming in her own way, I suppose, but exhausting."

"And Heather Winslow?"

"Just before lunch. She's writing another memoir, so she's always observing things. She's been wandering. Said she wanted to 'soak up the atmosphere.'"

"Who else is there?"

"There's Jonathan," she said.

"Mr Keats? Your housekeeper?"

She nodded. "He's been overseeing the staff. Making sure everything runs smoothly. Jonathan's very professional—he knows how to stay in the background."

"And the waitress who served us at dinner?"

"Just a local girl from the village," Lydia said, her tone softening. "Daughter of a friend. Seventeen—very sweet. She's been in the kitchen most of the night."

"Thank you," Atticus said. He steepled his fingers briefly, a gesture I recognised as him piecing together his thoughts. "That's all very useful."

"What now?" Lydia asked.

"I'd just like to have a quick chat with Jeremy in here, if that's all right."

"Of course. Do you need anything from me?"

"I'd like to speak to the guests individually. Is there somewhere that I could see them?"

"The snug," she suggested. "It's private and I think Jonathan left a fire in the grate."

"Perfect. I'll start with Simone and her husband—perhaps in ten minutes?"

"I'll speak to them now," she said, leaving us.

The door shut, leaving me alone with Atticus.

"Well?" I asked, crossing my arms. "What do you make of all that?"

Atticus moved to the desk, running his fingers lightly along its surface. "Simone and Richard are predictable. Early arrivals, loud and brash. Simone is exactly what she appears to be—ambitious, self-assured, and bitterly jealous of anyone she perceives as more successful than she is. She and Eleanor have been circling each other like rival cats since they arrived."

"Tom Grayson?" I asked.

"Salt of the earth. East End barrow-boy made good despite a few skeletons in his closet. I looked him up before I came here—he's done time for armed robbery. He's a bit of a handful. Attention-seeking. Loud. But more bark than bite."

"And Milo?"

"Debut novelist, big advance, but sales have been disappointing and he's feeling the pressure." Atticus paused, considering. "He's nervous and feels out of place. Someone who disappears and admits to needing time alone might be genuinely overwhelmed… or might have used the opportunity to take something from the study."

"Clara?"

"Screenwriter. Relentless. Ambitious, like Simone, but less combative."

I looked down at my notes. "Heather?"

"Memoirist. It's interesting that Lydia said she was wandering around the house."

"Might just be nosy."

"Maybe, maybe not. And Keats, the caretaker—he's been largely invisible. But someone who's always in the background might have seen something that others missed. We'll need to speak with him, too. The waitress is probably irrelevant, but we won't rule her out until we're certain."

Atticus gestured for me to join him by the French doors. "Look at that," he said, pointing to the faint trail of mud leading back towards the desk. "Someone opened these."

"Someone breaking in from outside?"

"Let's have a look."

He opened the door and stepped out into the garden, then took out his phone and activated the torch. He asked me to hold it and shine the light on the lock while he examined it. He leaned in close to the mechanism, his eyes narrowing.

"Shine the light here," he said, gesturing towards the area where the latch met the frame.

I obliged, watching as he traced the outline of the lock. He paused, tilting his head, then moved to inspect the doorframe itself, focusing on the section where the bolt would engage. He straightened and gestured for me to shine the light on the handle.

"Nothing obvious. No marks from tools, no signs of tampering. If someone opened it, they didn't force it from the outside."

"From the inside, then."

He nodded. "Either someone walked out with the contents of the safe, or they wanted it to look as though someone did. But at the moment, we don't have enough to say for certain."

"So what now? We speak to them?"

"Yes," he said. "Separately. Their movements, their alibis, their knowledge of the safe. Everyone here had opportunity, and I was at the same table as them tonight—they all had motive, too. You'll see when we speak to them. They're all hiding something, Jez. We just need to find out what."

3

The snug was in sharp contrast to the grandeur of the rest of the house, and its low ceiling and exposed wooden beams leant it an intimate, almost secretive air. The scent of aged leather and wood smoke lingered, mixing with a hint of pine from the garland draped over the mantel. A fire crackled in the hearth, the flames casting shadows that danced across the walls. Above the mantel hung an oil painting: a pastoral scene, its muted tones softened by years of smoke and heat. The hearth itself was flanked by two well-worn armchairs upholstered in deep green velvet, their fabric showing wear at the arms, with a leather Chesterfield facing them. The walls were panelled in dark oak and a brass lamp on a side table cast a warm glow, illuminating a stack of dog-eared paperbacks.

We sat down in the armchairs just as Simone Bradley and her husband Richard came inside.

"Take a seat," Atticus said, indicating the Chesterfield.

They sat: Simone with one leg crossed elegantly over the other, an air of studied relaxation about her, and Richard perched on the armrest. Simone wore a striking red dress, tailored to perfection, and a pair of diamond earrings that caught the firelight every time she turned her head. Richard was no less self-assured in dinner jacket and bow tie, a chunky Rolex showing on his wrist as he swirled the glass of brandy he'd brought with him.

Richard nodded at me. "Who's this?"

"My colleague," Atticus said. "Jeremy."

Richard offered a smile that didn't reach his eyes. "Pleasure."

Simone didn't acknowledge me, her attention fixed on Atticus. "I assume this is about the manuscript. I must say, the whole business is absurd. A theft? Here? Among us? It's unthinkable."

"It was in the safe and then it wasn't. If you have another explanation that'll tell us where it is, I'd like to hear it."

She shrugged. "I don't know. You saw what Eleanor was like at dinner—old and scatty. She put it down somewhere, and now she can't remember where it is."

"That seems unlikely," Atticus said. "I'd like to start with what you did earlier today. When did you arrive, and how did you spend the afternoon?"

Simone leaned back, crossing her arms. "We arrived before lunch. Lydia gave us the grand tour and then Richard spent most of the afternoon charming everyone in the sitting room, didn't you, darling?"

Richard smirked. "One does one's best."

"And you, Mrs. Bradley?" Atticus prompted.

Simone waved a hand dismissively. "Oh, mingling, catching up. Lydia and I had a lovely chat at one point—she wanted to show me some rare first editions she'd acquired."

"In the study?" Atticus asked.

"That's right—you've been there, I presume. It's where she keeps her library."

"We've seen it," Atticus said. "Eleanor said she put the manuscript back in the safe at half past three. Were you in there before or after that?"

Simone's smile faltered for the briefest moment. "After, I think. The safe was locked."

"How do you know that?" Atticus asked.

"The door was closed."

"How can you be sure it was locked?"

She paused. "True. I don't suppose I can be sure. I just assumed it was."

"Did you notice anything unusual? Anything out of place?"

Simone frowned. "Not that I recall. Though, to be honest, I wasn't paying much attention."

Atticus nodded thoughtfully, then shifted gears. "What about at dinner? How did you think it went?"

"It was interesting, I suppose. I haven't been invited to one of these before, and I probably anticipated it a little more than I should have."

Richard chuckled. "Simone's too polite to say it, but Tom Grayson was holding court. You saw how he is—always the loudest voice in the room. And dull as dishwater."

"And Eleanor?" Atticus asked.

Simone snorted. "She's *awful*. Aloof. Smug. But that's her to a tee, isn't it? She knows she's the star and makes sure you know it, too."

"The grand dame of literature," Richard added mockingly. "One book, thirty years ago, and dining out on it ever since."

"Don't misunderstand us," Simone said, turning back to Atticus. "I respect her work."

"Do you?"

"Of *course* I do. *Solstice* is a good book. Well—it's *worthy*. But you know how these literary types are—egos the size of planets."

There was an unspoken bitterness in her words, and I couldn't help but wonder how deep it ran.

"I heard the discussion the two of you were having," Atticus said. "I got the impression you don't think she takes you seriously."

"Well, she *doesn't*," Simone blurted. "Do you know how many books I've sold?"

"I know it's a lot."

"Ten million, all around the world, and I did it all *myself*. No publisher, no PR team, I don't even need an agent—I only have Lydia so she can sell film and TV rights. And do you know how many books Eleanor has sold?"

"I do actually," Atticus said. "I looked it up before I came here. Two million."

"Exactly. She sold half a million copies the year it came out and maybe another one and a half since then. *Two* million. I've sold five times as many books as her in the last ten years alone, but all I ever get from the likes of people like her are sneers."

"Ten million," Atticus said. "That really is a remarkable achievement." His gaze flicked over to her husband. "Mr. Bradley—you've been quiet. Anything to add?"

Richard shrugged. "Not much more to say, I'm afraid. From my perspective, the way Simone is treated by the likes of Eleanor is a disgrace. Simone's done more to encourage people to enjoy reading than Eleanor ever has—just *look* at all the good work she does in Wales. No one ever comments on that, and Simone's too modest to bring it up herself, but she supports libraries, sends books to schools… she brings *tourists* to the area. Do you ever see people like Eleanor doing anything like that? Of course you don't. They sit in their ivory towers, pecking away at their typewriters, waiting for inspiration to strike—Simone goes out and clubs it over the head."

"That's all very admirable and very impressive," Atticus said, standing. "You've both been very helpful. Thank you for your time. I may have more questions later."

Simone and Richard stood, too. There was a mirror above the fireplace, and as Simone turned to leave, I caught her reflection in the glass. Her polished smile had vanished, replaced by an expression I couldn't quite place: irritation, perhaps, or something darker. She noticed me looking at her and the practiced gloss returned like a mask.

I turned to Atticus as soon as the door had closed. "What do you think? Simone doesn't like Eleanor very much."

"It's more than professional rivalry," Atticus said. "It's personal. She resents her status, her critical acclaim. Simone will have had her fair share of rejection along the way, and, if you asked me to guess, I'd say she has a very large chip on her shoulder about it. For example: the conversation moved onto literary awards at dinner. Tom asked Simone if she'd ever won an award and she said she hadn't, and that she's not interested in them. She wasn't telling the truth, though. I think recognition from her peers is what she wants most of all. She has all the money she could ever spend, but she doesn't have Eleanor's cachet. Eleanor represents everything she feels excluded from."

"And Richard?"

"A loyal accessory," Atticus said. "He'll say what his wife wants him to say, no more, no less."

"Could they have stolen the manuscript?"

Atticus pursed his lips. "They have motive and opportunity." He paused. "I don't know. We need to speak to the others."

4

Milo was the next to join us. He stepped inside hesitantly, his slight frame seeming to shrink a little as he crossed the threshold. His dinner jacket, clearly expensive, hung awkwardly on him, as if it had been tailored for someone with broader shoulders. A mop of unruly brown hair flopped over his forehead; he brushed it away nervously, his hand trembling slightly. His pale complexion and the faint shadows under his eyes gave him the look of someone who hadn't been sleeping well.

"Mr. Priest," he stammered. He moved too quickly to the Chesterfield, bumping into a side table on the way. "This is about the manuscript?"

Atticus smiled. "It is. It's just a chat to see if you can help me work out where it is."

Milo nodded and sat. His shoulders hunched forward, and he clasped his hands tightly in his lap, his knuckles white. I watched as Atticus settled across from him.

"Why don't you tell us what you've been doing today?"

Milo gave a nervous nod, his gaze darting between Atticus and me. "Of course. Anything I can do to help."

"When did you arrive?"

"Um... eleven, I think," he said, his voice faltering.

"Is this your first time here?"

"I came last year," he said. "My book had just been signed."

"Lydia is Milo's agent," Atticus said for my benefit, even though I had already gathered that.

"She's been very kind. She took me on straight off the slush pile. No one else was interested in the book, but she saw the potential. I owe her everything."

"And after you arrived? What did you do this afternoon?"

"Well..." Milo hesitated, looking down at his hands. "I mostly stayed in my room. I'm not great with big groups. I get anxious. I unpacked, tried to get myself together, and then went down to the sitting room for a little while."

"Did you speak with the others?"

"Not much. I said hello to Lydia and spoke briefly with Heather. But mostly, I kept to myself."

"Why?" I asked, though the answer was obvious. "The anxiety?"

"Mostly that." He flushed, the redness creeping up his neck and into his cheeks. "Everyone here is so accomplished. So respected. And I'm... I'm just me."

"*Just* you?" Atticus repeated. "I think you're being a little unfair on yourself. Lydia wouldn't have taken you on if she didn't see something in you, and, for what it's worth, she was right. I've read *The Fragile Line*. It's excellent."

The way his smile broke across his face was almost heartbreaking. "You have?"

"I picked it up when it came out and I read it in one sitting. I thought it was wonderful. Very moving and beautifully written."

I knew Atticus was lying. I don't think I've ever seen him reading a novel and he certainly never mentioned that he'd read Milo's debut. He was seeking to establish a rapport between the two of them and Milo was so naïve—or so desperate for praise that he was willing to overlook the obvious—that he was happy to play along.

"That's very high praise," Milo said.

"Why do you say that?"

"To read it in one sitting—it's eight hundred pages."

"Fast reader," Atticus said deftly. "And especially when it's so well written."

Milo paused for a moment and, when he spoke again, the temporary infusion of happiness that had followed Atticus's compliment, had dissipated.

"It's lovely to get comments like that, but it almost makes things worse."

"What do you mean?"

"The book. You must have heard—it didn't do well. Everyone thought it would. The advance was huge, and there was so much hype, but then… the reviews. They were awful. And the sales…" He trailed off. "They were even worse."

Atticus nodded, indicating that Milo should continue.

"Do you want to hear something pathetic?" He continued before either of us could answer. "I've never seen anyone actually buy a copy in a bookshop. And it isn't as if I haven't tried. I've waited in shops for hours, hovering by the table where they kept the books and then—when they realised the books weren't selling and took them off the table and put them into the shelves—I've waited there. I've seen people pick it up, look at the cover, turn it over and read the blurb, and then put it back. That's what always happens. They put it back. I've never ever seen anyone take it to the counter or show even the slightest indication that they might be interested in reading it. It's so depressing."

"I can understand—"

I was trying to be sympathetic, but Milo wasn't listening. "I don't think Lydia will work with me again," he spoke over me. "She hasn't said it outright, but I can tell. And the others..." He gestured vaguely towards the rest of the house. "They don't respect me. I'm just the failed debut. The wunderkind who thought he could write and ended up embarrassing himself."

"No one said anything like that at dinner," Atticus said.

"They don't need to say it. I can tell."

Atticus let the silence stretch for a moment before asking, "You stepped away from the table for a bit, didn't you?"

Milo's flush deepened, and he fidgeted with the lapel of his dinner jacket. "I needed some air. It was warm in there, and I was feeling a bit... overwhelmed."

"How long were you gone?"

"Only a few minutes," Milo said quickly. "Maybe five? Ten at most. I stood on the drive for a bit, and then came back in."

"Did anyone see you?" Atticus asked.

Milo frowned, his brow furrowing as he thought. "I don't think so. Everyone was still at the table when I got back. I tried not to make a scene."

Atticus pointed to Milo's feet. "And the mud?"

Milo glanced down at his smart dress shoes, as if seeing them for the first time. "Didn't notice. It must have been from the edges of the drive."

"You didn't go into the garden?"

"No," he said.

Atticus gave a nod, his expression still unreadable. "And what about Eleanor? Did you notice anything unusual about her behaviour before the theft was discovered?"

He frowned thoughtfully. "She seemed distracted. But I don't really know her well enough to say if that's unusual. I know she's incredibly *well* respected and her first book was *so* amazing, but I wouldn't be surprised if she's beside herself with worry about the next one. There's a reason it's taken thirty years. The pressure to match *Solstice* must've been crushing. I don't think it's something I would've been able to manage."

"And the manuscript? Did she mention it to you?"

Milo shook his head. "No."

Atticus leaned. "Thank you, Milo. You've been really helpful."

He nodded, his relief almost palpable. "I hope you can work out what happened. It's all so… awful."

Milo left the snug, the door clicking softly shut behind him.

I turned to Atticus. "Well?"

Atticus raised an eyebrow. "He's nervous," he said, moving towards the fire and gazing into the flames. "Terrified, even. But not about the manuscript."

"No?"

"He's haunted by his own failure. That's all he sees when he looks at himself, and that kind of self-loathing is hard to fake."

"You don't think he took it?"

"I didn't say that. The mud on his shoes is bothering me. I'd like to have a look tomorrow morning and see if there are any footprints outside the door to the study. If there are, it'd be interesting to see if they match with his shoes. Simple enough to check. But still. Milo is a man drowning in his own insecurities. I wouldn't have thought he had the confidence to steal a glance at Eleanor's plate, let alone her manuscript."

5

The fire in the snug had burned low, and I was just adding another couple of logs when the door swung open, and Tom Grayson stepped inside. He entered with a confidence that bordered on arrogance and his dinner jacket was nothing short of a statement piece. Crafted from a deep burgundy velvet, it shimmered faintly under the light, exuding theatricality. The wide, peaked lapels were made of black satin, providing a glossy contrast to the richness of the fabric. A single button, also satin-covered, fastened the jacket neatly at the waist, accentuating Tom's broad shoulders and confident stance. The lining, visible whenever he moved, was a flamboyant paisley print in gold and crimson. He'd paired it with a crisp white dress shirt, a black silk bow tie, and flawlessly shiny black patent leather shoes. I would come to conclude that the ensemble reflected Tom's personality: bold, unapologetic, and designed to draw attention.

His weathered features still showed the charm that had made him a regular at book festivals and literary salons. Atticus had given me a little more about his background and

I could see why rooms of middle-class readers might find him so beguiling; he was a rogue, the edges smoothed away *just* enough for him to be respectable, but with a glint in his eye that suggested he was never going to be too far away from the 'naughtiness' he described in his gritty novels.

"Gentlemen," he said. "Lydia said you wanted a word."

"Please, take a seat," Atticus said, gesturing to the Chesterfield.

Tom sat, crossing one leg over the other with a casual confidence. "About the missing manuscript?"

"It is."

"Fire away."

"Let's start with the basics. When did you arrive and what were you doing before dinner?"

"Drove the Bentley," he said with a self-satisfied smirk, even though Atticus hadn't asked *how* he'd arrived. "Got here at half-ten. Spent most of the afternoon chinwagging with the others. Lots of polite chatter, very little substance."

"And Eleanor?"

The smirk widened. "She pretends I don't exist, and I enjoy reminding her that I do."

"What does she have against you?" Atticus pressed.

"She's perched on a very high pedestal, and people like me—people from my background—I don't think she appreciates that I get paid just as much as her for writing what she thinks is trash." Tom said it with a shrug. "You know she reviewed my first book?"

"I didn't."

"She didn't like it. She used Dorothy Parker's line—'This is not a novel to be tossed aside lightly. It should be thrown with great force.'" He chuckled. "I can laugh at it now, but it pissed me off something *rotten* at the time. My first agent told me something once, when I got started, just after I got out of stir: he said, 'never slag off another writer.' I never have and it's always served me well. Because, let's face it, I could've gone to town on her, couldn't I? If we're swapping fancy insults, I could've nicked Mark Twain's: 'A classic is something that everybody wants to have read, and nobody wants to read.' I could've said that her so-called 'genius' was a fluke, that *Solstice* only blew up 'cause someone waved it in front of Oprah, that my shopping list is a better read than anything she's done. But I didn't. Held my tongue. So now, seeing her wobble tonight, if you ask if I feel sorry for her, I'll tell you straight: I don't. Not a jot. She had it coming, mate."

It was a bravura denunciation and, judging from the way he leaned back with a smile on his face, he had enjoyed delivering it.

"Did you speak with her at all this afternoon?" Atticus asked.

"Barely," Tom replied. "A few words here and there. She was too busy basking in Lydia's adoration. It'll be the closest she's come to a spotlight in donkey's."

"And during dinner?" Atticus continued. "What was your impression of her then?"

"She was on edge—no question. Fidgeting, barely touching her food. Probably nerves—after all, it's been years since she's had to prove herself."

"Did you notice anyone leaving the table?"

"Milo slunk off at one point, but I've seen his type before."

"What do you mean?"

"Trust fund, uni, then off to North London to drink frappuccinos while sweating over how to make his sentences sing. I had a look at his Instagram bio before I came down to dinner—he's one of those they/them types, isn't he, doesn't know whether he's Arthur or Martha. I saw him skulking away and knew what he was doing."

"What was he doing?"

"Off to the bathroom to shove some gear up his schnoz."

"You think?"

"You *don't*?" He shrugged. "He looked like he wanted to crawl under the table for most of the meal and, when he came back, he was chattering non-stop. Draw your own conclusions. Other than that, everyone seemed glued to their seats."

I noted all this down.

"Let's talk about the manuscript," Atticus said. "When Eleanor announced it was missing, how did you react?"

"Surprised, of course. But I'd be lying if I said I wasn't also a little… entertained." Tom spread his hands. "The long-awaited sequel to a literary masterpiece, stolen during a dinner attended by the great and the good of the London literary scene—and me? It's practically a thriller waiting to be written. If I didn't know better, I'd say it was all staged for publicity."

"You think Eleanor staged it?" Atticus asked, his tone carefully neutral.

"No," he said. "She wouldn't have the savvy for that. Lydia, though? Different kettle of fish. She's always had a flair for the dramatic, and let's face it—nothing shifts books like a juicy scandal."

Atticus put his hands together. "Thank you, Tom. That will be all for now."

Tom stood, flicking an imaginary speck of lint from his jacket with exaggerated nonchalance. "If you want my tuppence's worth, you're flogging a dead horse here. It'll turn up eventually—things like this always do. But between you and me, she's better off if it stays buried. The critics will rip it to shreds, and I don't reckon she's got the bottle for that kind of drubbing anymore."

He left the snug, his footsteps echoing down the corridor.

I turned to Atticus. "Well?"

"He's confident," Atticus said.

"You think he's hiding something?"

"Not necessarily," Atticus replied. "But his confidence isn't rooted in innocence—it's rooted in his belief that he's untouchable. He thrives on provocation—makes him difficult to pin down."

"What he said about Lydia—she couldn't have taken it, could she?"

"Unlikely."

"So, where does that leave us?"

"With a room full of egos, rivalries, and secrets. The trick will be sorting the theatrics from the truth."

6

Eleanor Pierce was next, but we were waiting for fifteen minutes before she finally arrived. The door finally swung open, and she stood in the doorway looking flustered and close to tears. She was wearing a modest evening dress. Wisps of greying curls framed her sharp, birdlike face, her wide eyes passing nervously between Atticus and me.

"I'm sorry I kept you waiting," she said.

"No problem," Atticus said, gesturing to the chair.

She sat, her hands gripping her dress and twisting the fabric in nervous agitation. "This whole situation is dreadful. I can't imagine who would do such a thing."

"That's what I'm hoping to find out," Atticus said, leaning forward slightly, his hands clasped loosely. "Let's start with the manuscript. Tell me what you did with it since you arrived."

Eleanor swallowed. "I brought it with me," she said. "I arrived just before lunch, and Lydia showed me to my room. She knew I'd brought it—it's why I'm here, after all. She said it would be best in the study, in the safe. I agreed. She came with me. We opened the safe together and I locked it inside."

"You're certain it was locked?"

"Yes," Eleanor said firmly. "I checked it myself. Lydia even watched me do it."

"And no one else saw the combination?"

"Lydia set it—it's her safe, after all—and then she showed me how to use it. But no one else was there."

"So, to be clear—the manuscript was in the safe when you went to have lunch. But you took it out again afterwards?"

She nodded. "After lunch. I thought I might work on it. There are a few chapters left to polish, and I wanted to look it over before the reading. I went to the study, opened the door and took it out. I took it up to my room and worked on it there."

I noted all this down.

"What time did you bring it back to the study?"

"Around three."

"What did you do after locking it in the safe?"

"I went back to my room. I needed to rest before dinner. It had been a long journey, and…" She trailed off, her voice faltering. "And I needed a moment to collect myself."

"Lydia told me that it's all handwritten."

"It is. I've never been able to write with a typewriter, and a word processor is completely out of the question. I know it's superstition, but *Solstice* was written that way and it's always felt wrong when I've tried to do something different."

"And you've never made a backup?" I asked, genuinely curious. "Surely you've considered the risks?"

"Of course I have," she snapped. "Do you think I don't know how ridiculous it sounds? But I can't. I have to feel as if I'm making something special. Copying it would… I don't know, steal its soul."

"Did you go back to the study at any point before dinner?"

Eleanor shook her head. "No."

"And during dinner? Did you notice anything unusual?"

Eleanor frowned. "Not really. There was a lot of chatter, and people were... well, it felt like they were watching me. It felt like everyone was waiting for me to produce it."

"I'm sure they were all very excited."

"You don't know *anything* about my world," she said. "People take pleasure in seeing other people struggle. Publishing is full of jealousy and backbiting and gossip. I hate it. I'd be happy never to see any of them ever again."

Atticus eyed her carefully. "Anyone specifically?"

Eleanor's lips thinned. "Simone. My God. You were at dinner—did you hear some of the things she was saying? Passive-aggressive things about how long it's been since my last book. About how she could never take that long on a project because her readers would have moved on. Do you know how many books she published last year?"

"I don't."

"*Five*. Five books and they weren't short, either! Hundred thousand words plus. Do you know why? The platform she used has a model that pays by the word. I don't mean to be unkind, Mr. Priest, but she's a talentless hack. It's a production line of mediocrity. I had the misfortune of reading one of her novels—and I really do use that word advisedly—and it was like a *car crash*. I wanted to look away, but I just couldn't. It read less like a novel and more like a soap—formulaic, overindulgent, *no* depth. It's hard to believe anyone could stretch clichés so thin without them snapping entirely."

"You didn't respond to her."

"What was the point? I knew she was baiting me, and I wasn't going to give her the satisfaction."

"Tell me what happened when you went to get the manuscript."

"I went to the study. I opened the safe, it was gone." Her voice cracked on the last word, and she pressed a trembling hand to her mouth. "I thought I'd made a mistake, that I'd put it somewhere else and forgotten. But I haven't. I know I haven't."

"Is there anyone here you suspect might have taken it?"

Eleanor's gaze hardened. "Simone, perhaps. Or Tom—he's always had a grudge. He hates that I'm considered a serious writer while he's dismissed as commercial."

"He told us," I said.

"He told us about a review you wrote of his first book, too."

She rolled her eyes. "That still bothers him. My God—you'd think a man like him, with his background, would have a thicker skin. But no."

"Milo?"

"I don't see why he would. He's harmless. Wouldn't say boo to a goose."

Atticus put his hands together. "Thank you."

"That's it?"

"For now."

"Please," she said. "You've got to find it."

"I'll do my best. I'm confident I'll have an answer by the end of the evening."

We all stood.

"You must be proud of it," I said.

"The novel?" Her smile faded. "Proud? I don't know. Sometimes I think it's brilliant, and other times I think it's the worst kind of rubbish. That's the trouble with writing—you can't ever really be sure."

"Your readers seem confident," I offered. "There's been tremendous anticipation for the sequel."

"Faith is a dangerous thing. People expect so much. They build it up in their minds, and what if… what if it doesn't live up to that?"

Atticus nodded. "You're afraid of disappointing them?"

"Of course I am. Who wouldn't be? People don't wait thirty years for mediocrity. They want perfection. And what if I can't give them that?"

She left the room.

Atticus's gaze lingered on the closed door. "She's highly strung and deeply anxious. That much is obvious."

"Do you believe her?"

His expression was thoughtful. "I believe she's not telling us everything. The question is what is she leaving out and why?"

7

We stayed in the snug while Atticus conducted the remaining interviews. Clara Wainwright, the screenwriter, was brisk and no-nonsense. She stated plainly that she hadn't seen anything of interest during the evening and said that she had been with someone else who would be able to vouch for her ever since she had arrived at the house. Atticus told her he'd read she was upset that her pitch for an adaptation of *Solstice* had been rejected; Clara said she'd been fine with that, but not when key ideas she said she'd come up with had been included in the screenplay that was eventually filmed. But, as she said, 'that was years ago, and it doesn't bother me anymore.' There was a prickly irritation in her answer that made me wonder whether that was really true.

"She's the least suspicious of the lot," Atticus said afterwards. "It'll be easy enough to confirm her alibi, and, if it stacks up—and I don't really have any doubt that it will—it'll rule her out as the one who removed the manuscript."

Heather Winslow was a different matter entirely. The retired journalist turned memoirist admitted to wandering the house earlier in the day, claiming she had been 'seeking inspiration.' She went on in the same vein for five minutes.

"She over-explained her movements," he noted to me afterwards. "It's often as good as admitting guilt. I'd put decent money she was somewhere she shouldn't have been. The question is whether it was the study or somewhere else."

Both Heather and Clare were withering in their opinion of Simone and her husband. Heather suggested she was 'as self-serving as they come,' while Clare said Simone was jealous of Eleanor's success and despised the literary establishment that she clearly felt shunned her. Both confirmed, though, that at least one of them had been with the pair—save bathroom breaks—ever since lunch.

The two of us sat quietly in the snug while Atticus, with no shame or fear of being discovered, took out a packet of rolling papers and a bag of marijuana and started to roll another spliff. He fell silent, staring into the fire absent-mindedly as he rolled the joint between his fingers and thumbs. The flickering light cast shadows across his face, and I knew better than to press him further. He had a habit of letting the pieces arrange themselves in his mind, revealing patterns no one else could see.

We were still sitting there when Lydia appeared in the doorway. Her usually composed demeanour was rattled; her cheeks were flushed, and her lips were pressed into a tight line. Atticus had lit the joint, but she didn't mention it.

"Sorry to interrupt," she said, her voice clipped, though she was clearly holding back some urgency. "There's something you need to see."

Atticus stood. "The manuscript?"

"No," she said. "But I think we know who might have taken it."

8

We followed Lydia up the wide staircase and along the dimly lit corridor. The house had taken on an eerie stillness up here; the faint murmur of voices from the sitting room was almost entirely swallowed by the silence.

I noticed a man standing stiffly by one of the bedroom doors. He was in his late forties or early fifties, with the solid build of someone accustomed to manual work. His face, weathered and serious, betrayed discomfort. His arms were crossed.

"Jez," Atticus said. "This is Jonathan Keats. He works at the house."

"Jonathan takes care of things for me," Lydia added.

Keats shifted slightly, his discomfort evident. He gave me a brief nod but kept his focus on Atticus. "Inside," he said gruffly, jerking his chin towards the door. "You better have a look. I thought it best to leave things as they were."

Atticus stepped past Keats and opened the door. Lydia and I followed, the faint scent of beeswax polish mingling with the cool air of the room. The space was modest, functional rather than luxurious. A neatly made bed with crisp white linens was in the centre of the room. A small writing desk stood against one wall, its surface bare except for a lamp and a notebook.

The room was obviously the one that had been given to Simone and Richard. The bedside table held a hardcover copy of her latest novel—*In the Shadow of Snowdonia*—its gaudy, self-promoting dust jacket featuring her name in oversized embossed letters. A crystal carafe of water, flanked by two glasses, sat on a tray. A silk scarf was draped over the armrest of the chaise longue, and an open suitcase in the corner revealed impeccably folded designer clothing.

The bedside table held a vase of flowers, a jam jar filled with pens, a sheaf of papers and a bright yellow fountain pen.

Atticus paused just inside the room, his eye sweeping left and right before settling on the pen.

"This is Simone's room," Lydia said.

"I gathered that," Atticus replied. "What do you want us to see?"

Lydia pointed to the pen. "That's mine—a Parker Duofold in Mandarin Yellow. Very expensive. It's insured for ten thousand pounds."

Atticus smiled in disbelief. "Let me guess—it was in the safe?"

"It was. I didn't notice—my attention was on the manuscript, of course—but I just checked, and it was missing, too."

My stomach churned as I stared at the pen, its glossy surface practically glowing in the subdued light.

Atticus crouched to examine it. "You're certain it's the same pen?"

"Positive," Lydia said, crossing her arms tightly. "It was a gift from Martin Amis. There's no mistaking it."

Keats cleared his throat. "I found it there just before I called you."

Atticus stood. "And the manuscript?"

"No sign of it, sir. I checked the drawers, the wardrobe—anywhere someone might have stashed it."

"How thorough were you?"

Keats stiffened, his shoulders squaring defensively. "Thorough enough. I didn't want to make a mess, but I'm confident I would've found it if it was here."

"You mean you didn't want the guests to notice their rooms had been searched."

Keats said nothing. Lydia shifted beside me, her eyes flicking nervously between Atticus and the pen.

I gestured towards the bedside table. "Do Simone and Richard know you've found it?"

"I haven't told them yet," she said. "I thought it best to come straight to you."

Atticus nodded, his gaze lingering on the pen as though willing it to yield its secrets. "You did the right thing. No need to confront them prematurely."

I couldn't help myself. "What do you think it means?"

"It means," Atticus said, "that either Simone and Richard have some explaining to do, or someone wants us to believe they do." He turned to Keats. "You're sure no staff would have entered the room?"

Keats shook his head. "The housekeeper's been downstairs with me most of the evening. The girl from the village stayed in the kitchen. No reason for anyone else to come up here."

Atticus stepped back. "Good. Let's leave everything as it is for now."

"What are you going to do?" Lydia asked.

Atticus turned to Keats. "Have you checked the other rooms?"

"Yes—all of them. There's nothing to see."

"I wonder if you might leave me upstairs to have a look myself," Atticus said. He turned to me. "Do you think you could wait at the foot of the stairs to make sure no one comes up?"

"Yes," I said. "Of course. How long will you need?"

"Give me half an hour."

"What are you looking for?" Lydia asked.

"I'd rather keep my powder dry, if you don't mind. But I'm confident half an hour will be more than enough time for me to have the culprit and the manuscript."

9

The sitting room had a tense energy, the air thick with unspoken accusations and smouldering resentments, many of which had seen their temperature increased over the course of the last few hours. The fire crackled in the grate, casting long shadows on the walls, while the scent of mulled wine from the earlier festivities lingered faintly in the background and, somewhere, I could hear Bing Crosby singing 'White Christmas.' The guests were assembled, each of them sat on sofas or chairs, their expressions ranging from impatience to unease. Atticus stood by the mantelpiece, his hands clasped loosely in front of him.

I was sitting at the back of the room, my notebook in my lap, as I looked from person to person. Lydia Marchant, seated nearest to the fire, looked pale and drained, the earlier composure when she'd welcomed me into her home long since frayed. Eleanor Pierce sat stiffly with her hands clutched together in her lap, her face unreadable. Simone Bradley lounged on a sofa beside her husband, her posture deceptively casual, though I thought her eyes betrayed her unease. Milo Yates fidgeted—that was obviously his default—while Heather

Winslow and Clara Wainwright sat quietly, their gazes fixed on Atticus.

"Thank you all for your patience," he began. "I understand this evening has been deeply unsettling for all of you, but I believe we've reached a resolution."

He paused and looked around left to right, taking in the wary faces before him.

"To begin, let me recap the facts. The manuscript of *Equinox*, the sequel to *Solstice in September*, was reported stolen this evening. It was last seen by Eleanor when she placed it in the safe in Lydia's study earlier this afternoon. By dinner, it was gone, and with it, a valuable Parker Duofold fountain pen."

"A pen?" Tom interjected. "No one mentioned that before."

"It seems the thief was opportunistic and decided they'd take that, too," Atticus said. "The safe was locked and no one was seen to leave the house; those of you writing detective stories"—he inclined his head towards Simone and then Tom—"would no doubt call this a classic locked room mystery."

"Very Agatha Christie," Simone said.

"I've had the opportunity to speak with each of you, and what's become abundantly clear is that this theft is not as straightforward as it might appear. Everyone here has a motive—some more obvious than others. Eleanor, as some of you put it when speaking to me, is a polarising figure. She inspires admiration in some, jealousy in others, and outright disdain in the rest. And when you gather a group of people like you, with your egos and insecurities in close proximity, it's inevitable that grudges will bubble to the surface. Shall we go through them?"

"Do we have to?" Simone said, her lips were pressed into a thin line.

He turned to her. "You've made no secret of your feelings about Eleanor, have you? It was obvious just from what you said over dinner, and you made it even clearer when we spoke. You think she's a fraud, coasting on the success of a single book published decades ago. And you resent her for looking down her nose at you because you self-publish your novels, despite your significant commercial success. She dismissed your work—publicly, I might add—and I believe you hate her for it."

Simone opened her mouth to retort, but Atticus raised a hand, silencing her. He turned his gaze to Milo Yates, who shrank slightly in his chair.

"The young prodigy. Plucked from obscurity and handed a hefty advance on the strength of his debut. A book that, unfortunately, didn't live up to expectations. The critics savaged it, sales tanked, and now you're terrified you'll never publish again. You see Eleanor as a symbol of what you'll never achieve—real literary prestige and an enduring career."

Milo stammered, "I-I'd never—"

Atticus cut him off, shifting his attention to Tom. "The provocateur. Your relationship with Eleanor is… antagonistic. You enjoy mocking her. Dismissing her as a relic while ensuring she knows you haven't forgotten her. But your digs aren't just playful barbs. Her reputation as a literary darling irritates you because it's a pedestal you've never quite reached, and never will reach. You look at literary London and know a man of your background—with your baggage—you'll always be a curiosity, someone brought to events like this because you're 'colourful.' You'll always be an outsider, and Eleanor is the ultimate insider. She's everything you'll never be."

Tom smirked, but it was strained. "Flattering as that is, Priest, I'm not in the habit of stealing notebooks."

Atticus moved on without acknowledging the interruption. "Clara," he said, turning to the screenwriter, whose carefully neutral expression didn't waver. "You've spent years trying to pitch adaptations of other people's work, including Eleanor's, but she refused you outright. She dismissed your vision, claiming it wasn't 'true to her story.' You saw the success she achieved with the adaptation of *Solstice*, and you've always suspected that she used the notes you provided her when you pitched for the job without her permission."

Clara raised a single brow. "If you think I'm petty enough to sabotage a manuscript over a rejected pitch, Mr. Priest, you haven't spent much time in Hollywood."

Atticus nodded, acknowledging her deflection, then turned to Heather.

"A journalist who made her name writing about the tragedies of others. And yet, here you are, struggling to make your memoirs sell. What better boost to your career than to have been present at the theft of the literary world's most anticipated manuscript? It'd make an excellent story—one you'd no doubt enjoy being at the centre of."

"That's a desperate reach," she said.

Atticus shrugged helplessly. "Yes," he said, "I think so too, but it's the best I could come up with on short notice. You'll be pleased to hear that I know it wasn't you."

Finally, Atticus turned to Eleanor, who was sitting stiffly in her chair, her face pale. "And Eleanor Pierce," he said. "The one common denominator in all of these grievances."

The room fell silent, all eyes shifting to Eleanor, who visibly swallowed but held her ground.

"But who is responsible for the theft?" Atticus turned to Simone. "Let's start with you."

Simone raised an eyebrow, her lips curling into the smirk that I had come to associate with her. "Of course. Why not me first?"

Atticus ignored her sarcasm and reached into his pocket. He withdrew the canary yellow fountain pen and held it up. "As I said—this pen was also taken from the safe. It wasn't reported missing until half an hour ago."

"I didn't notice it was gone," Lydia explained. "My attention was on the manuscript."

"Understandable," Clara said.

"Whatever," Simone said. "What does it have to do with us?"

Atticus eyeballed her. "It has a lot to do with you. It was found in your room."

Simone's eyes widened, her polished façade fracturing for the first time. "In our room?" she said, her voice climbing an octave. "That's ridiculous. Why would it be there?"

Richard shot to his feet, his face flushed with anger. "You've got some nerve. Are you trying to pin this on us?"

The other guests shifted uncomfortably in their seats. Milo looked down at his lap, Heather exchanged a wide-eyed glance with Tom, and Clara raised a hand to her chest as though steadying herself.

"Surely not," Clara said. "Simone, Richard—you wouldn't…"

"Of course we wouldn't!" Simone snapped, her cheeks flushed. "This is absurd. Why would we steal a bloody fountain pen?"

"It's not the pen, though," Lydia said. "It's the manuscript. Whoever stole the pen most likely stole that."

Eleanor stood up, too. "Where is it, Simone? Where is my manuscript?"

"We didn't steal the pen," Simone said with exaggerated patience. "And we didn't steal the manuscript. I have no idea why that would be in our room."

"Sit down, please—both of you." Atticus remained unflappable, his gaze steady as he looked between them. "That's exactly the question, isn't it? Why would it be in your room? Why would anyone leave such a valuable—and incriminating—item in plain sight for us to find?"

Simone opened her mouth to respond but closed it again, her expression flickering with confusion. Richard's fists clenched at his sides. "Someone's trying to frame us."

"Yes," Atticus said calmly, lowering the pen. "I believe that's exactly what's happened. The pen was planted in your room. It was placed there because whoever stole the manuscript knew how much bad blood there was between Simone and Eleanor, and they rather simplistically assumed it would point the finger squarely at Simone."

A murmur rippled through the room.

"Planted?" Tom said. "By whom?"

"I'll get to that," Atticus said. "But first, let me demonstrate why neither of you could have been responsible. I've put together a timeline of the afternoon's events. Eleanor says the manuscript was removed from the safe between the time she says she put it back—three-thirty—and the time she went to get it for the reading—nine-thirty. To have gone from the sitting room, where you both were for most of the afternoon, to the study, then back to your room before returning to the sitting room, would have taken five minutes, and that's not even considering how long it would have taken you to open the safe, assuming, of course, that you knew the combination—and I'm not convinced anyone knew that beyond Lydia and Eleanor. But during that time both of you were in the sitting room, engaging in conversations witnessed by at least three other people. Furthermore, the presence of the pen in your room makes no sense. Why would you steal the manuscript and then leave an incriminating piece of evidence in plain sight for me to find? It's clumsy, and neither of you strike me as clumsy. Finally, I observed your reactions when I questioned you and your confusion then and your obvious outrage now are inconsistent with guilt and more aligned with being framed."

I watched the room closely as Atticus spoke. Simone's indignation had given way to something else; exhaustion, perhaps, or relief that she and Richard were no longer under the microscope. Richard, meanwhile, sat rigid, his fists clenched on his knees as though ready to lash out.

Atticus, however, was unshakable. He held the Parker Duofold aloft like a magician revealing a crucial prop. "This pen," he said, "was a deliberate misdirection. Whoever took the manuscript wanted to divert suspicion away from themselves."

There was a ripple of discomfort around the room. Tom leaned back, an amused smirk tugging at his lips, while Milo squirmed, avoiding everyone's gaze.

Atticus turned it slowly, the firelight glinting off its bright yellow barrel. "So, who would gain the most from such a misdirection?"

He paused, his gaze sweeping across the room before settling on Eleanor.

I caught the faintest flinch; a subtle twitch of her shoulders, as though Atticus's words had struck a nerve. In that moment, I felt the temperature shift, or maybe it was just my own pulse quickening.

"I said earlier that you are a polarising figure, and that everyone here had a reasonable motive to want to see you suffer. But the irony is, it wasn't their motives we needed to focus on. It was yours."

Eleanor's pale face was now tinged with a faint blush.

"Is there anything you'd like to say?"

"No," she said quietly.

"Perhaps in private? I'd be happy to spare you the embarrassment of explaining what happened in front of everyone else."

"Of course not," she said. "I have nothing to hide."

Atticus nodded; I thought he looked a little sad.

"I'm afraid I looked in your room before I came down here." He took an envelope out of his pocket, opened it and tipped the contents onto the floor. A handful of ash tumbled out, fine and grey, with faint black specks scattered through it. "I scooped this out of the grate in your room. At first glance, it might seem unremarkable—ash in a fireplace in December, after all, no big surprise there. But there were several things about it that were rather unusual. First of all, I don't believe anyone else had a fire upstairs today. This house might be old, but it is warm. There are digital thermometers in the rooms, and I asked Mr. Keats to download the temperatures in yours from today. It's been a steady twenty-two degrees, so I do find it rather strange that you would need to light the fire."

"I get cold," she protested.

"Well, yes, but then I wonder why you haven't worn anything warm all day"—he gestured towards her dress with the bare shoulders—"especially when you have a suitable cardigan in your wardrobe."

"You've looked through my wardrobe?"

"I'm afraid I thought it was necessary. The temperature and your outfit both suggest there would have been no reason for a fire to be lit. Unless, of course, there was something specific to burn."

"I lit a fire because I was cold. This is ridiculous."

"What did you burn?"

"Wood, of course."

Atticus tipped the remaining ash from the envelope into his palm. "Ash from paper and ash from wood are quite distinct if you know what to look for. Wood ash is denser, coarser, and often contains larger, grainy pieces of unburned material, like bits of bark or fibre. Paper ash is lighter, almost feathery, and tends to crumble into a powdery residue." He put some of the ash between thumb and forefinger and rubbed, grinding it even finer. "The colour is another giveaway—paper ash is a pale grey, sometimes with a hint of white, while wood ash is darker, with more earthy undertones. The ash here clearly points to something more delicate than a log or kindling—something much more likely to be paper. And then there's these."

He brushed the ash off his palm, reached into his pocket again and took something else out. He held out his fist, turned it over and opened it: we all saw two small, charred metal bars.

"The ends of a treasury tag," he explained. "Small stationery fasteners consisting of a pair of metal ends connected by a sturdy piece of string, often used to bind loose pages together. The string has burned away, but these are made of brass, and they've just discoloured a bit."

Lydia stared at Eleanor. "You used treasury tags to hold it together—I remember."

She glanced away.

Atticus put the tags back in his pocket. "You admitted that you opened the safe to remove the manuscript, but I don't believe you put it back. I suspect you intended to review it, perhaps make some final adjustments, but something changed.

Perhaps it was anxiety, or the weight of expectation. Whatever the reason, you made a choice—to destroy the manuscript rather than risk it being read and found wanting. You decided to burn it and then, realising that you would have to say something, you went back to the safe, took out the pen and left it in Simone and Richard's room."

Eleanor's hands trembled slightly, and she pressed them harder into her lap. "That's absurd."

Atticus stepped closer, his tone softening. "Is it? You told me yourself how terrified you were of disappointing your readers. Thirty years is a long time to carry the weight of a masterpiece. You said faith was dangerous—that you couldn't be sure if the book was brilliant or terrible. In the end, fear won. You decided not to take the chance."

The room fell silent, the crackling fire the only sound. Eleanor's shoulders sagged, and she looked down at her lap, unable to meet anyone's gaze.

"Eleanor," Lydia said. "Is this true?"

She didn't answer at first. When she finally spoke, her voice was hoarse. "I didn't mean to… I didn't think... I was desperate."

"You could've come to me, Eleanor. We could've handled it."

"There was nothing to handle!" Eleanor snapped, her composure breaking. "The manuscript wasn't good enough. It would never be good enough. Everyone wanted another *Solstice*, and I couldn't give it to them."

Tom chuckled. "And instead, you gave them this. A scandal that will eclipse anything *Equinox* might have achieved."

Eleanor's head dropped further, and she began to weep.

10

Atticus turned to Lydia. “I believe that concludes my work here. I’ll be heading home—my dog will need to stretch his legs before he goes to bed.”

Atticus bowed his head to the others and made his way out into the hall.

Lydia and I followed.

“Thank you,” she said.

Keats arrived with our coats.

“Thank you for inviting me,” Atticus said. “It was a very interesting evening.”

“I’ll be in touch,” she said. “I’m very confident I’ll be able to find a home for your book.”

I said goodbye to Lydia and followed Atticus outside. He glanced back at me, a faint smile playing on his lips.

“That was unexpected.”

The two of us stepped outside into the crisp night air, the stars bright above the frost-covered grounds. A fox darted across the far edge of the grounds, its red coat vivid against the pale landscape.

I looked at my watch; it was coming up to half-past two. Christmas Eve had become Christmas Day without me even noticing.

"Not the Christmas Eve I expected," I said, pulling my coat tighter.

Atticus turned his collar up against the chill and smiled faintly. "But one we'll remember," he replied. "Happy Christmas, Jeremy."

"Jez."

His eyes flashed with mischief.

THE CASE OF THE BOLTED DOOR

1

I was balanced at the top of a stepladder with a roller in one hand and a tray of paint in the other when the doorbell rang. It was a Monday morning in late August, and the Winchester office of Priest & Co wasn't looking its best. The walls were half-painted, with the magnolia I'd chosen clashing against the dark green left behind by the previous tenants. Dust sheets covered most of the floor, leaving just enough space for us to shuffle around, and the faint smell of turpentine hung in the air. A pile of unopened boxes—stationery, files, and a coffee maker that I still hadn't set up—was stacked haphazardly in the corner.

After weeks of cajoling Atticus Priest into helping me decorate the two rooms I'd arranged to rent, he'd finally agreed to come over to help. I knew he wouldn't be well suited to the task, but I wanted him to visit so I could demonstrate how seriously I was taking my new responsibilities. So far, his contribution had been limited to stirring the paint tin and offering unsolicited advice about how much faster it would go if I'd just 'get someone in to do it properly.' I probably *should* have done that—and, dear reader, it would only take me spilling a pot all over the floor to make the requisite call—but I wanted to show my new employer some frugality and a can-do attitude. I have come to realise that neither of those qualities are ones Atticus is concerned about, especially not when he is presented with the kind of mind-bending problem as was about to be the case.

The task had not been made easier by the fact that he'd brought his dog to the office, and I'd brought mine. The two of them had never met before; Bandit, a German short-haired pointer, was a little older than my Treacle, and, while I'd imagined that seniority might have meant he took charge, Treacle disagreed. He was an eight-month-old Goldendoodle with firm ideas about his status in the pack and a store of energy that had so far proven to be limitless. The two dogs were standing with their paws on the windowsill in the smaller room—the room where I'd shoved the second-hand furniture that I'd bought from Facebook Marketplace—and were barking excitedly at anyone and everyone who passed by on the street below. The radio was playing loud, but the dogs were more than a match for Winchester Radio's nostalgic throwback to the 1980s, drowning out Annie Lennox as she sang about what 'Sweet Dreams' were made of.

"It's the bell," Atticus said.

"Could you get it?" I called down to him.

"I'm busy," he said, turning his phone around so that I could see the chessboard on the screen.

"Not as busy as I am," I said, showing him my paint-stained hands.

He sighed and went to the door. He returned a moment later with an inquisitive look on his face. "We have a visitor."

A woman followed him into the office: mid-thirties, with sharp features softened by a faint smile. Her dark hair was pulled into a tidy ponytail, and her sensible grey suit suggested someone who valued practicality over flair.

She looked up at me and smiled. "Jez."

I smiled back. "Lucy?"

"Haven't seen you for a while."

I started down the ladder. "Not since I jacked it in at the newspaper."

"I heard. What was *that* all about?"

I took a rag from the bottom rung of the ladder and wiped my hands. "Got bored. Fancied a change."

"To private investigator?"

I shrugged, still feeling the usual tinge of embarrassment that I had the audacity to call myself that. It had the same sort of out-of-the-ordinary quality as astronaut or deep-sea diver, and—to this child of the nineties, anyway—brought to mind David Jason as DI Jack Frost or John Nettles as DCI Tom Barnaby.

She ignored my discomfort and turned to Atticus.

"You must be Atticus."

"I am," he said. "How'd you know that?"

"You're becoming well-known," she said. "And we're not that far from Salisbury. Your reputation goes before you."

I finished wiping my hands and tossed the rag aside. "Lucy is a—"

"Hold on," Atticus said, holding up his hand to stop my introduction. He kept his palm upraised as he made a show of considering her. "Lucy is a detective constable."

Her eyes went a little wider. "How can you possibly know that?"

Atticus smiled, I hadn't known him for long then, but I knew how much enjoyment he derived from showing off. This was an opportunity to do that.

"Your shoes are polished to a mirror shine but scuffed around the soles—appearance is important, but you put in a lot of miles. Your ponytail is secured with a scrunchy, functional rather than decorative, and there are faint indentations on your scalp from wearing it tightly for long hours. It's the kind of style chosen for practicality, especially when you're on the move. And the ID holder tucked just slightly into your jacket pocket, which you've tried to hide but can't help fiddling with, tells me you're used to carrying credentials. Combine that with the way you immediately assessed this room when you walked in, that you know who I am and that I suspect you've come here to ask for help, and police work seems inevitable. Your age—mid-thirties, I'd say—suggests detective constable is most likely." He smiled. "How did I do?"

Lucy blinked, caught between surprise and amusement. "Not bad."

"Not bad?"

"I'm a DS, not a DC. Detective Sergeant Lucy Trimble."

She put out her hand, and Atticus took it. "Nice to meet you."

"Likewise."

I felt I ought to explain our relationship for Atticus's benefit. "I got to know Lucy when I was a journalist," I said. "She worked on a couple of investigations I covered and was always good enough to tip me the wink when there was something I ought to know."

"That's sort of why I'm here today," she said. "You're right. I am looking for help, and I was sort of hoping Jez would be able to introduce me to you. The fact that you're here is… well, it feels like good timing."

"Propitious," Atticus said, his smile widening just slightly, the faintest glimmer of satisfaction in his eyes. "I'm flattered."

Lucy chuckled, brushing a strand of hair from her face. "Do you have fifteen minutes?"

"Of course," he said, his antennae clearly twitching. "But not here. The smell of the paint is giving me a migraine."

"And the dogs aren't helping," I said, indicating the second room, where they were still doing their duty and warning us whenever anybody went within range of the window.

"They need a run," Atticus said. "Perhaps you'd like to come? Walk and talk? You can tell me whatever it is you think I might be interested in on the way."

Lucy glanced toward the smaller room and nodded. "That sounds perfect."

2

The sun was warm, and the roads around the cathedral were bustling. Bandit and Treacle tugged at their leads, eager to sniff every tree, bench, and bush. Lucy walked between me and Atticus, a smile on her lips as she glanced at the dogs. The office was at number 83 on the High Street, and it was just a five-minute amble to the cathedral and not that much farther to the open spaces around the Itchen.

"They're a handful," she said, nodding toward Bandit, who was busy trying to untangle himself from Treacle's lead.

"Bandit's the calm one," I said. "Treacle's a work in progress."

We crossed Loverose Way and wandered out onto the lawn on the northwestern side of the cathedral.

"So," Lucy said. "Thanks for hearing me out."

"Pleasure," Atticus said. I glanced over at him and could see a glitter in his eyes that I'd come to recognise as a sign of his interest in something that he thought could be exciting. "You've got my attention. What is it you'd like to ask me?"

"It's a case I've been working on."

"Right."

"A sudden death. Something about it doesn't sit right."

Atticus gave a nod, his pace slowing as he let Bandit lead him toward the cathedral. "I'm all ears."

"The dead woman's name is Alice Carmichael," Lucy began. "Late forties, very well off, big house on Sleepers Hill. Found two days ago in her locked and bolted bedroom."

"Cause of death?"

"The initial theory is anaphylaxis after eating something containing nuts."

I frowned. "Did she know she had a nut allergy?"

"She did," Lucy confirmed. "Very severe. She'd had it all her life, and, because of it, she was *extremely* cautious about what she ate. But the suspicion is that her brother Richard deliberately gave her something to trigger it."

"Deliberately?" Atticus said.

"I know what that means," she said.

"That'd make it murder," I added redundantly.

"What was it?" Atticus said.

"What did he give her? A brownie."

"Death by chocolate?" I suggested, then immediately wished I hadn't.

Lucy let my remark pass with nothing more than a disapprovingly raised eyebrow. "The brother—Richard—he's actually quite well known."

I remembered the name. "Richard Carmichael? He won *Bake Off* last year?"

"That's right."

"*Bake Off*?" Atticus frowned. "Never heard of it."

It was still early in our professional relationship then, and I hadn't yet discovered Atticus's complete disdain for most popular culture (save his love of chess and prog rock, although it would be a stretch to call either popular). "*The Great British Bake Off*," I explained. "It's a baking competition on the TV. Contestants bake ridiculous things in a big tent in the garden of a country house. My ex-girlfriend loves it."

The truth was that *I* enjoyed it, too, but I decided to keep that to myself.

"Sounds awful," Atticus said.

"Richard has a colourful backstory," Lucy said. "He did ten years for armed robbery and learned how to bake when he was inside. It's rags-to-riches stuff. Everything has changed for him now—he's had a bestselling baking book, and companies pay him very well for endorsements. He visited Alice the day she died and brought her a tray of brownies. Nathan, their other brother, said it was a peace offering. There's been a long-standing feud in the family over their late mother's estate, particularly the house Alice and Nathan live in. The three of them had arranged to discuss it—to see if they could find a way to resolve the dispute."

"I see," Atticus said. "And the locked bedroom?"

"Nathan says Alice was paranoid after a burglary last year. A couple of chavs broke in and stole valuables from her bedroom while she was asleep. Freaked her out—totally understandable. She spent a fortune equipping the house with a high-end security system—cameras, motion detectors, all that—and she'd also started locking her bedroom door at night. When she didn't come down for breakfast the next morning, Nathan called the police. The attending officer forced the door open and found Alice dead in bed. There was a half-eaten brownie on the floor."

Treacle gave a tug on his lead, and I stopped to untangle him from a lamp post. I caught up with them. "So Nathan's pointing the finger at Richard?"

"Very much so," Lucy said. "He says Richard knew about her allergy and included nuts deliberately. We searched Richard's house and found hazelnuts in his bin. It all seems damning, but…"

"But something about it doesn't feel right," Atticus said, finishing her thought.

"Exactly," she said. "It doesn't. Nathan seems almost too eager to blame Richard. You know what it's like sometimes—you just get a gut feeling."

"You do." Atticus was quiet for a moment, his gaze fixed ahead as Bandit stopped to sniff at a patch of grass. "What about the post-mortem?"

"Preliminary results *suggest* anaphylaxis. Fluid build-up in the lungs and cardiovascular collapse. But it's not conclusive."

"Toxicology?"

"Still pending."

Atticus nodded thoughtfully. "Interesting. And Richard? What does he say?"

"He insists his brownies were nut-free," Lucy said. "He admits they'd been rowing and that he knew she had an intolerance, but he swears up and down that he'd never hurt her. But the evidence we've found makes it difficult to dismiss the possibility."

"You've questioned both brothers?"

"We have."

"But no arrests?"

"My DCI wants me to bring Richard in again. The CPS think they have enough to charge, but they just want us to get his answers to a couple of extra questions."

Atticus stopped walking. "I'd be happy to take a closer look. I consult for the police in Salisbury—would you like a similar arrangement?"

"I'm not sure my gaffer would be up for that. Could we keep it quiet for the moment and see how we get on?"

"Of course. I'll need more details. Full access to the post-mortem report, and I'd like to have a look at the bedroom. And I'll need to talk to the brothers, of course."

Lucy's smile widened. "I'll make sure you get everything you need."

3

We went back to the office to drop off the dogs and then set off again. The Carmichael house was in Sleepers Hill, just a mile away from the High Street and in one of the more affluent areas of an already affluent city. It was a striking property, all clean brickwork and symmetry, with white stone detailing framing the large windows and a columned portico guarding the front door. The detached garage to the right had the same elegant finish, its slate roof mirroring that of the house's.

"This is nice," I observed.

Lucy pressed the button for the intercom.

"Cameras," Atticus said while we waited, noting the two cameras focussed on us.

The speaker buzzed. "Hello?"

"It's DS Trimble," Lucy said. "Do you think I could have a word?"

"Of course. I'll buzz you in."

The gate opened, and Lucy stepped through, making her way to the door, where she pressed the discreet doorbell. A faint chime echoed inside, and after a moment, the door opened to

reveal Nathan Carmichael. I would have guessed that he was in his mid to late forties, with a lean and angular build. His face was elongated with sharp cheekbones, a high forehead, and an aquiline nose, giving him an air of intelligence. His green eyes stood out, and his hair was neatly styled. He also looked every inch a man struggling under the weight of grief: his face was pale and shadowed with sleeplessness, he didn't look as if he had shaved for a day or two, and his clothes certainly hadn't seen an iron.

"Mr. Carmichael," Lucy said, her voice professional but warm, "how are you?"

"I'm doing okay," he said. "How can I help?"

"This is Atticus Priest," she said. "And this is Jez Hardwicke. I've asked them to help with the investigation into your sister's death."

"Are they police?"

"No," she said. "Atticus is a private investigator."

Nathan paused before his face lit up. "Atticus Priest? From Salisbury?"

"That's right," Atticus said.

Nathan shook Atticus by the hand. "This is a surprise," he said, smiling. "I read about you after the case at the cathedral. The man who fell from the tower."

Atticus was always pleased to receive praise, but, today, I could see that he was more interested in getting inside the house to look around.

"I'm hoping Atticus might be able to help us confirm what happened," Lucy said.

"That would be wonderful," Nathan said. "Please—all of you, come in."

We followed him inside, and I took the opportunity to glance around: polished wooden floors, subtle recessed lighting, and a faint scent of furniture polish in the air. It was the kind of house that shouted wealth and good order, every detail carefully curated. Cameras were mounted discreetly in the corners of the hallways. I looked up the property when we returned to the office later and found that it had been purchased by Nathan's parents, off plan, for three million. It had probably accrued even more value in the time since.

Nathan took us into the kitchen and sat on one side of the dining table while the three of us sat opposite. His hands were clasped tightly. The room was as immaculate as the rest of the house: the polished oak surface gleamed under the soft overhead light, a vase of fresh lilies sat perfectly centred, and there was not a speck of dust on the furniture. The faint scent of citrus polish lingered in the air.

Nathan cleared his throat. "How can I help you?"

"I'd like to hear what happened at your meeting with Richard and Alice."

Nathan exhaled. "Alice wanted us to meet. She said it was important that we talk everything through face-to-face. That was her—always the one trying to keep the peace."

"And this was about your mother's estate?"

"Yes. Mum passed away last year. Left this house to Alice, which Richard and I weren't happy about. Not because we wanted to take it from her—well, not exactly—but because it felt unfair. The house is worth a fortune. If it were sold, the money could have been divided evenly between us. Instead, Alice got everything, and Richard and I got… scraps."

"Scraps?" Atticus asked.

Nathan waved a hand dismissively. "Some savings, a few stocks, nothing close to the value of this place. Alice always said Mum gave it to her because she was the one who stayed here and looked after her in her last years. Which is true, I suppose. But still… it didn't sit right with either of us."

"So the meeting was to resolve the dispute?"

Nathan nodded. "That was the idea. Alice wanted to convince us to drop it. She said she'd buy us out if she could, but she couldn't afford to right now. Richard was angry about that—he said she was just making excuses. Things got heated."

Atticus leaned forward. "How heated?"

Nathan hesitated. "There was shouting. Mostly between Richard and Alice."

"And you?" Atticus asked. "Where were you in all this?"

"I tried to keep things civil," Nathan said. "I told them there was no point in fighting. But Richard… he's always been volatile."

"Volatile how?"

Nathan looked at Lucy. "Did you tell him about…?"

"The armed robbery?" Atticus said.

Nathan nodded. "He got ten years inside for that. That was where he learned how to bake. Got out and reinvented himself—winning the *Bake Off* was massive, but it was just the start. There was the cookbook, the TV appearances, the whole works. But his temper never went away. He's good at hiding it on camera, but behind closed doors… it's a different story."

Atticus's expression didn't change. "What happened after the argument?"

"Richard stormed out," Nathan said. "Said he'd had enough and wasn't going to waste any more time talking to us."

"When was this?"

"Around nine," he said.

"It's on the cameras," Lucy confirmed. "Ten past nine."

"Alice and I stayed up for a bit longer," Nathan said. "She was upset, but she said she wasn't going to let Richard bully her into selling. We both went to bed around eleven."

"And the next morning?"

Nathan swallowed hard. "I got up around six, like usual. Alice didn't usually get up until eight, but eight came and went, and I noticed she hadn't come down yet. I knocked on her door, but there was no answer. I called her name—still nothing. That's when I started to worry."

"So you called the police," Lucy said.

"Yes," Nathan said. "Her door was locked *and* bolted from the inside. The constable had to break it down. And then, when we got in…" His voice faltered, and he looked away.

Atticus gave him a moment before speaking again. "I'm sorry to ask, but…"

"She was lying in bed," Nathan said quietly. "Looked like she was asleep. But she wasn't breathing. And then I saw the half-eaten brownie on the floor next to the bed. I put two and two together."

Atticus tapped his fingers lightly on the table. "And then?"

"The officer told me to wait outside," Nathan said. "The paramedics came and confirmed she was dead."

"PC Flynn attended," Lucy confirmed. "I can let you see his report."

"I told him about the brownie," Nathan said. "It was either an accident or deliberate, but he knew about her allergy. She nearly died when we were kids. It's not something he could've forgotten."

"Deliberate, then?" Atticus said.

"I think so."

"PC Flynn informed the SIO," Lucy said, "and it was decided it might be suspicious. A forensic team attended, and then the coroner was informed."

"They took the brownie," Nathan said.

"Alice didn't eat anything Richard had brought during the meeting?"

"No. They were in a box—wrapped with a bow. We'd started to argue before she opened it."

Atticus let that settle, and I spent the moment of silence watching Nathan. He didn't look outwardly suspicious, his posture was tense but not overly defensive, and his body language was open. His eyes flicked between Atticus and Lucy—rightly dismissing my importance—yet there was something in the set of his jaw, the way his fingers tightened momentarily on the edge of the table, that hinted at unease. I was interested in finding out what Atticus made of him.

"Tell me more about Richard," Atticus said. "You said he had a temper?"

Nathan nodded. "Always has. Even when we were kids. He was the golden boy, the one Mum doted on, but he had this edge to him. When things didn't go his way, he'd lash out. The robbery wasn't a one-off. It was the culmination of years of bad behaviour."

"And yet he turned his life around," I said.

Nathan snorted. "You could call it that. He got lucky. He lied when he applied to go on *Bake Off*. He didn't tell them he'd been inside, and it was only after they started filming that it all came out. It was in the *Mail*. There was a lot of fuss, but he'd already made an impression by then. He was popular, and then he won it all. He's good at what he does, I'll give him that. But don't let the cameras fool you—he's still the same person underneath."

Atticus tilted his head. "Capable of murder?"

Nathan met his gaze. "I wouldn't have said so, but what do I know?"

Atticus leaned back in his chair, his fingers steepled in front of him. "Thank you."

Nathan blinked, clearly taken aback by the abrupt shift in tone. "That's it?"

"For now," Atticus said. "But I may have more questions later."

Nathan nodded. "Whatever you need."

"Do you think I could have a look in your sister's bedroom?"

4

Nathan led us upstairs, past a wall-mounted security panel with glowing lights and stopped in front of a door that had evidently been forced. "This is Alice's room," he said, his voice tight. He corrected himself. "*Was* her room."

Lucy glanced at him. "You're sure you don't mind us taking a look?"

He shook his head. "No. Not if it helps work out what happened."

His voice trailed off, and he stepped back, letting us pass.

Atticus went inside first. I followed, with Lucy close behind me, her notebook already in hand.

The bedroom was immaculate. A large bed dominated the centre of the room, its white duvet still neatly arranged except for one corner where it had been pulled back. A bedside table stood to the left, its surface empty save for a lamp, a small stack of books and an EpiPen in a sealed plastic case. The windows were fitted with thick, motorised blinds that were partially drawn. The only thing that was out of place was the door; the wood around the lock had splintered,

jagged edges sticking out like broken teeth; and the bolt hung awkwardly, bent from the impact. The frame itself bore the scars of urgent entry, with scuff marks where a shoulder or foot had done the deed.

Atticus went to the door and inspected it. "Made a bit of a mess," he said. "You didn't have a key?"

"No," Nathan said. "Alice had the only one, and she kept it bolted, too."

"I can see that," Atticus said, pointing to the remains of the bolt.

Lucy pointed to a spot near the head of the bed. "The brownie was there. Half-eaten. As if she'd dropped it."

"Has it been analysed?" Atticus asked.

"Yes," Lucy replied. "Initial tests confirmed the presence of nuts—hazelnuts, specifically."

Atticus nodded absently, his gaze shifting to the bedside table. He looked at the books, then the EpiPen in its case. He stared at it, his hand going to his face and scratching absentmindedly at his cheek. He went to the window, running a finger along the frame. He inspected the glass. "Double-glazed. Tightly sealed. No drafts, no ventilation. Locked, too. And a good, sturdy lock."

I stepped closer, noticing the small motion sensor mounted near the top of the window. "The security looks thorough."

"It is," Nathan said from the doorway. "We were burgled last year. They came in here while Alice was asleep. She insisted on upgrading everything afterwards: cameras, motion detectors, locks. Everything."

"The window lock was secured?" Atticus asked.

"Always," Nathan said.

"I saw the security cameras outside before we came in. One of them looked as if it covered this window. Has it been checked?"

"Yes," Lucy said. "We reviewed all the footage—inside and out. No one went anywhere near the window. No one went in, and no one came out. The door, too—Alice came inside at just after eleven and didn't come out again. The door was forced at eight thirty."

"Interesting," Atticus said.

He turned back to the room, his eyes scanning every detail: the furniture, the untouched carpet. He crouched down to examine the gap between the bed and the wall. He ran his fingers along the floor, then straightened, brushing off his hands. He stepped back toward the centre of the room, his gaze lingering on the inset lights in the ceiling. The plaster had been chipped around one of the bulbs.

"Have you noticed something?" I asked.

He didn't answer immediately.

"Atticus?"

He looked down and shook his head. "The cameras, the locks, the double-glazed windows… the security is significant."

Lucy frowned. "So what do you think?"

Atticus took a moment to reply. "I'm not sure. I'd definitely like to see the post-mortem report."

"I can email it across when I get back to the station."

"Please do." He looked back at Nathan. "Thank you for letting us see the room."

Nathan looked as though he wanted to ask something, but he stopped himself, stepping back to let us leave.

We reconvened with Lucy outside the house.

"What do you think?" she asked.

"I have some questions. Too early to say anything now. I would like to speak to Richard, though. Can you arrange that for me?"

"Of course. He's in St. Cross Road."

"That's a half-hour walk," I said.

"Want to see if he's around now?" she asked.

"No time like the present."

5

Lucy received an urgent call from the station during the walk and excused herself from our visit to see Richard Carmichael. She'd called ahead, and after what sounded like a tricky conversation, he had apparently agreed to see Atticus and myself.

"He can be prickly," she warned us.

"I'm not surprised," Atticus said. "He probably thinks you're about to charge him with murder."

Lucy said that she would be in touch later in the afternoon, and we parted ways.

* * *

Richard's house was a far cry from his late sister's modern home. It stood in a quiet, leafy street, a red-brick Edwardian semi-detached with an air of understated charm. The façade was framed by a low brick wall and a neatly clipped hedge, with a wooden picket gate that creaked as we passed through it. The front garden was small but well-tended, with a few shrubs and a tree whose branches cast dappled shadows on the gravel path leading to the door. Large sash windows had white frames that were freshly painted, and the slate roof sloped gently, broken only by a tall, thin chimney stack.

It was the kind of place that suggested quiet success, tasteful but not ostentatious. I couldn't help but notice how carefully maintained everything seemed. It was all neat and ordered, and my amateur psychology suggested that it could have been a reaction to the time that Richard had spent behind bars.

The man himself opened the door before we could knock. I saw the family resemblance with Nathan, but Richard had a rugged, weathered appearance that suggested he'd seen things

his brother had not. His face was round with pronounced cheekbones and deeply carved lines. His short, tousled dark brown hair was unkempt, as was his beard. He was wearing an apron, and his hands were covered in damp flour. He didn't look like someone who'd done ten years for armed robbery; he was more Heston Blumenthal than Reggie Kray.

"You must be Mr. Priest," he said.

"I am. And this is my friend Jeremy Hardwicke."

He nodded at me.

"Call me Jez," I said.

"Jez." Richard nodded. "You're here about Alice."

"We are," Atticus said evenly. "Thank you for agreeing to meet with us."

Richard stepped aside, gesturing for us to enter. The interior was just as polished as the exterior, with dark wooden floors and walls lined with framed photographs of culinary triumphs: Richard shaking hands with other chefs, holding awards, and posing in the kitchens of what I assumed were high-end restaurants.

He led us into a bright kitchen that was dominated by a marble-topped island. Flour dusted the surface, mingling with scattered measuring spoons and a rolling pin that looked like it had just been used. A mixing bowl sat to one side, filled with a glossy batter, and the faint hum of the oven hinted that something was already baking. The air was rich with the scent of chocolate and butter, warm and inviting. The trophy from his win on *Bake Off*—a decorative crystal plate—was displayed on a large wooden dresser.

Richard motioned for us to sit at the island, while he remained standing, leaning slightly against the counter.

"Before we begin," he said, crossing his arms, "let me make one thing very clear. I didn't kill Alice."

"Then I'm sure you won't mind answering a few questions."

"Happy to. The whole thing about the brownies… it's the most ridiculous nonsense I've ever heard. You must see that."

Atticus leaned back slightly in his chair and adopted a conversational tone. "Let's start with them, shall we? You brought them to the meeting—correct?"

"Yes," Richard said. "We've been rowing for months, and I wanted to get things off on a friendly footing."

"To sweeten the mood," I suggested.

"Exactly. And Alice always loved my brownies."

"Did she eat one that night?"

He shook his head. "We started arguing before she even had a chance to open the box."

"And the recipe?" Atticus asked. "Would you mind showing it to me?"

Richard moved to a drawer near the oven, pulling out a small black notebook. He flipped through the pages before sliding it across the island. "There. That's the one I used."

Atticus picked up the notebook, skimming the recipe. I leaned over to glance at it as well. The ingredients were handwritten in precise, blocky letters: flour, sugar, cocoa powder, eggs, butter; nothing unusual. There was no mention of nuts.

"Are these the only brownies you make?" Atticus asked.

"Almost exclusively. They're a crowd-pleaser, and they're easy to make." He nodded at the crystal plate. "I used that same recipe when I won that."

"And you're *certain* there were no nuts involved?"

"One hundred per cent. Her allergy to nuts was extreme. She nearly died when she was a child, and she's been very careful ever since."

"Nathan told us about that."

"You've spoken to him?"

"We went to have a look at the house," Atticus said.

"What did he say?"

"Nothing at odds with what he told the police."

Richard's jaw stiffened. "He's a lying bastard. You can't trust *anything* that comes out of his mouth."

Atticus let that pass. "Tell me about the meeting with your siblings."

His expression darkened as he folded his arms. "It was tense."

"Who suggested it?"

"Alice did. She wanted to talk about the house—wanted to make peace, she said, but that wasn't going to happen. Nathan and I were both angry. I told her it wasn't fair, her getting everything while we were left with scraps. She said she understood how it stung, but she wasn't to blame for that. Mum made the decision. Nathan backed me up at first, but he always does that—lets me take the lead, then swoops in to play the reasonable one. Alice stood her ground, said Mum wanted her to have the house because she'd cared for her." He sighed. "That's when it all went wrong. She shouted, I shouted, Nathan shouted. I said some things I probably shouldn't have, but Alice gave as good as she got. In the end, I couldn't see the point in staying, so I left."

Atticus tilted his head. "What time was that?"

"Around nine," Richard replied. "Alice was still fuming. Nathan said he'd try to smooth things over, but who knows what he was *really* up to." He gave a bitter laugh. "That's the last time I saw her—alive, anyway."

"Nathan said he came to see you the morning Alice's body was found."

Richard nodded. "That's right. Around ten thirty."

"How was he?"

"He looked upset—genuinely shaken."

"What did he say about the brownie?"

"He said he'd found one of them, half-eaten, on the floor next to the bed, and had I put hazelnuts in it. I told him the same thing I told you."

"What about the nuts the police found in your bin?"

Richard's jaw tightened. "I didn't buy hazelnuts, and, even I did, I'd never use them in something I made for my sister—not then, not ever. I have no idea how they ended up in my bin, but it wasn't me who put them there."

He got up, went to the oven, and opened it. The most delicious smell swept out: warm chocolate mingled with the subtle, nutty aroma of browned butter. A freshly baked chocolate tart, its glossy surface cracked slightly from the heat, sat on the middle rack.

"Can I tempt you with a slice?" he asked, pulling on a pair of oven mitts and carefully lifting it out.

"It would be rude to refuse."

I said I'd like a slice, too, and we watched as he took a knife and sliced neatly through the tart, the blade gliding through the dense filling. He placed two delicate slices on small ceramic plates, handing one to me and the other to Atticus. I took a bite, and the rich, bittersweet chocolate melted on my tongue.

"Good?" Richard asked.

"Very," I said through a mouthful.

"You know the saddest thing about all of this?" Richard said. "I walked away from the house that night, and I decided I'd let things stand as they were. I've done all right after I got out—I have this place, I've got enough money to be comfortable, and I actually like what I get to do with my days. I told myself I was probably being greedy, and it wasn't worth the aggravation. I decided I'd sleep on it to make sure I was sure, and then, if I was, I'd give Alice a call in the morning. I woke up the next day, and I hadn't changed my mind. I was just making a cup of tea, and then I was going to call her, and then Richard came round and told me what had happened."

Atticus put his fork down on the plate. "Do you think Nathan would ever have felt that way?"

"Not a chance," Richard said bitterly. "When he didn't get what he wanted, he took it personally. It was him who started pushing Alice to sell the house so we could split the money. She refused, of course, and they had a falling-out over it."

Atticus stood. "Thank you for your time, Richard. You've given me a lot to think about."

"That's it?" Richard asked.

"For now," Atticus said. "But I may have more questions later."

6

Winchester was warm and pleasant as Atticus and I strolled back toward the city centre. The dogs had been in the office for a couple of hours and would need a chance to relieve themselves and stretch their legs.

Atticus's phone buzzed, and he paused, pulling it from his pocket. He scanned the screen, his expression unreadable.

"What is it?" I asked.

"The toxicology report from the post-mortem," he said, still focussed on his phone. "Lucy has sent it."

We were next to an empty bench in the grounds of the cathedral. Atticus sat down, and I did the same.

"And?" I prompted.

He frowned slightly, turning the screen toward me. "Take a look."

I shook my head. "I don't speak medicalese. You'll have to translate."

"Alice had elevated histamine levels, which *could* suggest an allergic reaction. But it's not definitive. Histamine can also be elevated post-mortem for other reasons, especially if there was stress or physical trauma before death."

"Physical trauma?" I asked, frowning.

"Not necessarily the kind you'd expect in a violent attack. Something as minor as a coughing fit could theoretically cause it."

"So… anaphylaxis *isn't* ruled out?"

"Correct," he said. "But it isn't confirmed, either."

"Isn't anaphylaxis obvious? Swollen airways?"

Atticus nodded. "In many cases, it is. But there's no mention of significant swelling in Alice's throat or airway in the report. The pathologist notes mild inflammation, but that's not conclusive on its own. If it *was* anaphylaxis, it should've been more pronounced. That's one issue. The other one is more of a problem. There were no traces of nuts in her stomach."

"That doesn't make any sense at all."

"Not in her stomach, not in her oesophagus. If she ate something containing nuts, it must have been such a small amount that it left no trace. And that's… unlikely."

"But not impossible?"

"No," he said. "Unlikely. You know what else was strange? She didn't use her EpiPen."

"It was on the bedside table," I said.

"Unused. I checked. And according to the report, there's no puncture wound consistent with an auto-injector on her body."

"Maybe she didn't get the chance?"

"Maybe," he said, though he didn't sound convinced.

We stood up and resumed walking.

"If it wasn't anaphylaxis," I said, "what was it?"

Atticus glanced at me, his expression thoughtful. "That's the sixty-four-thousand-dollar question, isn't it? The symptoms don't add up. If it wasn't an allergic reaction, then we're looking at something else entirely. Something less obvious."

"Come on, Atticus," I pressed. "You can't just leave me hanging."

He slowed his pace. "Let's assume for a moment that Alice didn't die from an allergic reaction. What else could cause similar symptoms—respiratory distress, cardiovascular collapse—without leaving obvious signs in an autopsy?"

I thought for a moment, then shook my head. "No clue."

"Carbon monoxide."

I stopped again, staring at him. "Carbon monoxide? Like from a car exhaust?"

"Or a faulty appliance. It's odourless, colourless, and *extremely* dangerous in enclosed spaces. And it can mimic the symptoms of anaphylaxis—dizziness, confusion, respiratory failure."

"Wouldn't the toxicology report pick that up?"

"Not necessarily," he said. "Carboxyhaemoglobin levels in the blood are the definitive indicator of carbon monoxide poisoning, and the pathologist wouldn't test for it if they were focussed on an allergic reaction. It's not standard unless there's reason to suspect it."

"And do we have reason to suspect it?"

He didn't answer immediately, his gaze distant. "Not yet. But the airtight room, the lack of definitive evidence for anaphylaxis, the unused EpiPen… they all point to the possibility of something more calculated."

"And Nathan?" I asked.

"He found the body," Atticus said. "He's the one who pushed the narrative around the allergy. And he's the one who came to see Richard in person. Why didn't he call him to tell him what had happened?"

"He said—"

"Yes, yes—it's the kind of news that needs to be delivered in person. That's very convenient. It would also give him the perfect chance to leave the offending packaging somewhere it would be found."

"You think he did it?"

"I think," Atticus said carefully, "that we need more evidence. He had the motive. He had the opportunity. The means is more difficult, but I do have an idea how he might have got around it."

We reached the High Street, the chatter of shoppers and tourists rising around us. Atticus tucked his phone back into his pocket, his pace quickening.

"Are you going to tell me what happened?"

"No," he said. "I need to be sure before I do that. You'll think less of me if I'm wrong."

He took out his phone again and called Lucy. He said she should ask the pathologist to test for carboxyhaemoglobin, and then, once she'd done that, to join us at Nathan's house.

"So that's where we're going?" I said, hurrying to keep up. "To see Nathan again?"

"It is," he said. "And I'm going to need you to do something for me."

7

Nathan opened the door before we knocked, his face tight and pale, a wary look etched into his features. "Back again?"

Atticus offered an apologetic smile. "I appreciate your patience. Just tying up a few loose ends."

Nathan's hand tightened on the doorframe, as if debating whether to let us in. Then, with a forced smile, he stepped aside. "Of course. But I really don't see what else you can possibly need to know. I told you everything."

We followed him inside. The house was as immaculate as before, but there was a tension in the air that hadn't been there during our previous visit.

Nathan hovered by the stairs, his arms crossed defensively. "So, what is it this time?"

Atticus glanced at me, our prearranged signal. "I've got a couple of extra questions, but, before I get to them, do you think it would be possible to use the facilities?"

Nathan nodded. "Of course," he said, pointing. "First door on the right."

"Thank you," he said. "I won't be a minute."

"Do you think you could put the kettle on?" I asked, following Atticus's instructions. "I haven't had a coffee all day, and I'm gasping."

If Nathan was suspicious at our requests, he made no reference to it. "Of course," he said. "This way."

Nathan turned and made his way to the kitchen, with me following behind. I risked a quick glance back and saw that Atticus, after pausing by the door to the bathroom, quickly continued along the hallway to the stairs. I heard the faint creak as he put his weight on the first tread and started up to the second floor.

* * *

Our requests might have been innocuous, but Nathan's suspicion returned when Atticus still hadn't rejoined us even after the kettle had boiled. I'd done my best to distract him, but it had been no easy task; his affability had disappeared, and now he had the air of a man who didn't trust anyone, his eyes flickering constantly back toward the hallway.

"Where *has* he got to?" he said, shifting uncomfortably.

I didn't have the chance to reply before Nathan's head snapped toward the hallway. A faint creak—Atticus's weight on the floorboards upstairs—had given him away.

"Where is he?" Nathan demanded, turning on me. "What's he doing?"

"In the bathroom," I said, trying and failing to sound convincing.

"No, he *isn't.*" Nathan's face darkened. "He's *upstairs.*"

He stormed past me, heading for the corridor.

How long had it been? Six or seven minutes at best, Atticus had said he wouldn't need long, but I had no idea whether that would be enough.

By the time I caught up with Nathan, he was already up the stairs and halfway along the hall. He threw open the door to the second bedroom, where Atticus stood calmly by a wood-burning stove, his hands clasped behind his back.

"What the hell are you doing in here?" Nathan barked, his voice shaking with anger and, I thought, panic.

"Looking for answers," Atticus said simply.

"This is my bedroom!" Nathan shouted.

"I know."

"It's *private*."

Alice's bedroom, directly below this one, was neat and tidy and minimal. Nathan's, on the other hand, was not. It was a chaotic jumble of mismatched furniture, an overflowing laundry basket, and stacks of papers that teetered precariously on every available surface. The bed, unmade and draped with a faded duvet, sat at an angle, as if it had been pushed aside hastily. An empty mug and a half-eaten sandwich sat forgotten on the bedside table, and the faint smell of stale coffee lingered in the air. The stark contrast to Alice's orderliness was striking, and Atticus's eyes lingered on the disarray with interest.

Nathan was still fulminating angrily. "You can't just—"

"I think I've found what I was looking for," Atticus interrupted.

I surreptitiously reached into my pocket, took out my phone and tapped the screen to start recording a voice memo.

The tension in the room was thick enough to choke on. Nathan stood rigid, his fists clenched at his sides, while Atticus remained composed, his gaze fixed on the wood burner. It was a standard cast-iron model, the kind you'd expect to find in any well-appointed home.

"The modification wasn't professional," Atticus said. "Crude, but effective."

"What modification? What are you talking about?"

Atticus crouched down and pointed to the base of the flue, where the pipe connected to the stove and vented smoke into the chimney.

"There are scratches on the metal," he said, his eyes narrowing as he traced the edges with his fingers. "It looks like the flue was removed. And *here*—do you see this circle of discolouration on the top of the stove? I think this is where a temporary cowl was attached. The tape you used has lifted up the dirt and dust."

"A *cowl*? What?"

"With an opening at the top where you fitted a hose," Atticus continued. "What did you use? If it were me, I'd use something like a salad bowl with a hole cut into it to slide the hose through, then use tape to make the hole airtight and to attach the bowl to the top of the stove. Crude, but effective."

"I'm confused, Atticus," I said.

"There's no need. This'll help."

He stalked across the room, crouched down next to a large and slightly dirty rug, grabbed it by the edges and yanked it back, exposing the floorboards beneath. He went from board to board until he found the one he wanted.

"Here," he said, pointing.

He looked around the room, saw what he wanted—a knife that had been left on the desk—and reached up for it, pushing the blade between the boards and then prising it back. Nathan started to protest and took a step towards him, but, before he could get there, the end of the board popped up, and Atticus yanked it all the way out. He put down the knife and took out his phone, activating the torch and shining the light down into the void between this floor and the ceiling of the room below: Alice's room.

"I noticed it when we were down there earlier," Atticus said. "Jez, you'll remember—there are inset down-lighters in the ceiling. Right? The plaster around one of them had been disturbed as if it'd been popped out and then put back again, but causing a little bit of cosmetic damage in the process. I suppose it was something of a gamble on my part, but once I'd seen the post-mortem and I was sure it wasn't anaphylaxis—and most likely something like carbon monoxide poisoning—I started to wonder about how the deed might have been done. You already told us that your bedroom is directly above Alice's, and when I realised what the loose fitting might mean, it started to make sense. I downloaded the floor-plan from when Alice bought the house and saw that each bedroom has a stove, like this one."

"This is absolute nonsense," Nathan protested, but even I could see that Atticus was making him very anxious.

"I think it happened like this," Atticus said. "You used this stove to produce carbon monoxide. It's an easy enough process—you starve the fire of oxygen, and it begins to produce the gas instead of smoke. You'd removed the flue, put a cowl over the stove outlet and fitted a hose into an opening in the cowl. That hose came across the floor and into the cavity, passing through the hole where you'd removed the downlighter. It vented the gas directly into Alice's room, and, since the room was airtight—double-glazed windows, a door that snugly fits the frame, no ventilation—it meant the gas would quickly build to lethal levels. I doubt the constable would have noticed the downlighter was missing, and, even if he had noticed, why would he have suspected anything given the cause of death looked obvious. You put it back when you had the room to yourself."

I realised my mouth was hanging open. I looked at the screen of my phone to make sure it was still recording.

"I suspect you lit the stove and got the process started late at night, knowing Alice would've locked her door and gone to bed. It wouldn't have taken long. A good plan, I'll admit—carbon monoxide is odourless, colourless, and undetectable unless someone knows exactly what to look for—but you were just a little sloppy. You should've moved the EpiPen, too. If she really *was* suffering from anaphylaxis, she would've at least tried to use the pen. It's unlikely that the shock would've come on so quickly that she didn't have the chance to do that. But she didn't. It was still in its case, unused. The reason for that, when you think about it, is obvious—it *wasn't* anaphylaxis, and the gas would've meant she never even woke up."

"And the brownie?" I said.

"That was quite deft. I think Nathan probably baked a batch before the meeting and would've had one of them ready to leave in the room. Is that right? You waited behind the police constable when he forced the door, knowing that the officer's attention would have been on the bed, and then dropped the brownie and pointed it out. I wouldn't be at all surprised if the packaging found at Richard's house was the same packaging from the hazelnuts that *you* used. Of course, there were two benefits of framing Richard: firstly, it'd lessen the possibility that suspicion would fall upon you and, secondly, it'd remove the other potential beneficiary to the will. Alice would be dead, Richard would be back in prison, and you'd inherit everything. It was a carefully crafted narrative, one designed to misdirect everyone, and it very nearly worked."

I turned to look at Nathan. His face had drained of colour.

"*Madness*," he said. His breathing quickened, his chest rising and falling. "This is *absurd*. You have no proof."

"That's the thing, though." Atticus shrugged. "I kind of do. And I've asked for a more detailed toxicology report to confirm it. Elevated carboxyhaemoglobin levels in your sister's blood, consistent with carbon monoxide poisoning, and no other easily explicable way the gas could've found its way into the bedroom.

You've probably dumped the hose somewhere, but I bet there'll be evidence from when you bought it—a receipt, something in your bank account. And then there's your behaviour—the way you planted evidence to frame Richard, the suspicious visit to his house the morning after her death rather than calling him. The money you stand to make. It all fits, Nathan. It sounds outrageous, but when you put it all together, it's the only explanation that makes any sense."

Nathan took a step back, his gaze darting between Atticus and me. For a moment, I thought he might try to argue, to deny it all. But then his shoulders sagged, and the fight seemed to drain out of him.

"She always thought she was *better* than me," he said, his voice barely above a whisper. "Always looking down her nose at me, like I was nothing. And Mum—Mum gave her everything. What did I get? Nothing. Nothing but scraps."

"You killed her over money," Atticus said, his tone devoid of sympathy.

"No," Nathan snapped, his eyes blazing with sudden fury. "I killed her because she deserved it. She deserved to know what it feels like to lose."

The confession hung in the air, heavy and bitter. For a moment, none of us moved. Then, as if a switch had been flipped, Nathan bolted, shoving past me and tearing down the hallway.

"Nathan!" I shouted, stumbling after him.

But he was already gone, the sound of the front door slamming echoing through the house.

"Don't worry," Atticus said. "He won't get far."

8

Atticus was right: Nathan *didn't* get far.

The scene outside the house was chaotic by the time we got down there. Atticus had called Detective Sergeant Lucy Trimble, and she was waiting by her unmarked car, her arms crossed. Two uniformed officers had intercepted Nathan and were restraining him, one man on either side.

Nathan looked as if he was going to faint. "This is ridiculous! I didn't do anything!"

"You can explain everything down at the station."

She gestured to the officers, and they moved him to the waiting car.

"I didn't kill her!" Nathan protested. "It was Richard—he brought the damn brownies!"

"It's a bit late for that," Atticus said. He turned and waited for me to hold up my phone so that Nathan could see that I'd been recording the conversation. "We have your confession. You're just wasting your breath."

Nathan glared at Atticus, and then, for the second time, the fight drained out of him. Lucy told the two officers to take him

to the station, and he didn't resist, meekly ducking his head and sliding into the back of the patrol car.

We watched until the car disappeared and then joined Lucy on the pavement outside the gate.

"You were right," she said. "The toxicology report has come back. It was carbon monoxide."

I turned to Atticus. "You weren't sure?"

"Sure enough," he said with a wink.

Atticus summarised the key points for Lucy's benefit: Nathan's motive was financial: his mounting debts and resentment over Alice's control of the estate. The method was simple but effective: producing carbon monoxide using the wood burner in his room and venting it into Alice's airtight bedroom through a hose threaded via a downlighter. The cover story was built around Alice's severe nut allergy, with a planted brownie and hazelnut shells pointing the finger at Richard. But the one slip-up that gave him away was the misaligned downlighter, a small imperfection that might well have been missed if it weren't for Atticus's keen eye for detail.

"You've made my job a lot easier," she said.

Atticus inclined his head. "The evidence will speak for itself. I doubt you'll have any problems. You should call the station and have a couple of SOCOs sent down to search the house. He was confident enough in himself and his plan to the point of hubris. I wouldn't be at all surprised if he was arrogant enough to have left evidence around the house. You'll be looking for a hose and a bowl with a hole cut into the bottom."

9

Death by Chocolate. I'm a little ashamed to admit that I gave a moment's thought to using that as the title for this entry into Atticus's casebook. Atticus, treating these accounts with the same amused disdain now as he did when I told him about them, suggested *A Recipe for Disaster* and *A Bitter End*. I decided against all of them on the basis that they were a little flippant and disrespectful, given that someone did actually die—was *murdered*—and because it felt a little... well, a little *Midsomer*.

The case against Nathan Carmichael quickly became unimpeachable. The SOCOs sent to search the property found a mixing bowl in a garden shed with a hole cut into the bottom, a roll of heat-resistant tape and a length of rubber hose. The bowl hadn't been washed and still had traces of the doughy mixture that Nathan had used to make the brownies. Nathan said he'd never seen the items before and, six months later, pleaded not guilty at his trial at Winchester Crown Court. The evidence—together with the confession I'd recorded—was too much for him to overcome, and the jury found him guilty by unanimous verdict. He was sentenced to fifteen years imprisonment.

Richard Carmichael was absolved of any guilt. There was great interest in the case among the tabloids—whose sub-editors did not share my qualms when it came to how they headlined their reports—and Richard's own fame continued to grow. His first book raced back to the top of the bestseller list, and he was able to parlay his fame into a much-improved advance for his second. And, of course, with the death of his sister and the incarceration of his brother, he inherited the entirety of the Carmichael estate. We didn't speak to him again, but a month after the verdict, a courier delivered a box to me in the Winchester office. It was fastened with a ribbon, and the accompanying card, signed by Richard, thanked us for our help. I opened the box and found that he'd baked us a batch of his acclaimed brownies. They contained hazelnuts and were delicious.

And, for us, Atticus's success in solving an unusual murder was useful in establishing the new office. Lucy Trimble would return with other problems that had vexed the authorities, and enquiries from locals keen to engage us would mushroom to such an extent that the problems of capacity Atticus was facing in Salisbury would also come to affect us here. But those are stories for another day.

For now, I reflect on what made this case stand out. It wasn't the locked room in which Alice was murdered, though that was certainly a puzzle worth solving. Nor was it the meticulous planning Nathan had employed in an attempt to kill his sister and frame his brother. What has lingered in my mind was the way family ties could twist into knots so tangled, so poisoned, that they became impossible to unravel. For all his planning, Nathan's downfall wasn't the damage around the bulb in Alice's bedroom; it was his arrogance in thinking that he could outsmart everyone, including Atticus.

Because as he so often reminds me, there's no such thing as a perfect crime. And yet, every time we step into a case, I find myself marvelling at just how close some people come.

THE HAUNTING OF HALLOWS HOUSE

1

The office was quiet on the morning we were introduced to the Carringtons and the baffling series of events that threatened to drive them out of their new country retreat and back to London. I'd been nursing a lukewarm coffee for the better part of an hour, and Atticus had been busy with his online chess. It looked as if he had three games of blitz on the go; he tabbed across to one of the open windows, analysed the position and made his move, chuckling with evident satisfaction before switching to the next in line.

I'd been working with him for two months at that point, and we'd settled into a comfortable rhythm. There had been plenty of work, both in the Salisbury and Winchester offices, so much so that Atticus had started to muse on the benefits of expanding into Bath. He'd gone as far as looking at the price of rental property and had, for the moment at least, decided to build up what we had a little more. We would eventually find suitable premises, and it would be me who moved west to open our third office, but that would only happen after the conclusion of the Lockerly investigation, and that—

and the very serious legal trouble that would be coming my way in particular—was still a month away.

Atticus had asked me to come over to Salisbury for an appointment with potential new clients. He wouldn't tell me their identity, saying only that it was a husband and wife with considerable wealth at their disposal and a problem that they'd been almost too embarrassed to discuss when he'd spoken to them. That was intriguing, of course, and I'd decided it must have been a family issue: blackmail, perhaps, or something involving a child. Atticus smiled at my suggestions and, when I asked if I was warm, replied that I was so cold as to be practically frigid, and told me I was going to have to wait. I dropped off my dog with my mum and dad and drove west.

I was just considering a second coffee run when the knock came from the door downstairs: a hesitant, three-tap rhythm.

"Here they are." Atticus minimised the windows with the chess. "They're nervous."

I got up and went down to the door to let them in.

A couple stood in the passageway. The man, in his early thirties, was tall and lean, his dark hair neatly styled. He wore a black turtleneck and jeans and black boots that looked extremely expensive. The woman beside him, of a similar age, was dressed in a beige coat that must also have cost a fortune. Her blonde hair was pulled into a ponytail, and a silver crucifix was visible in the V of her shirt's neckline. The two of them looked polished and had the air of a power couple, their wealth obvious but not ostentatious; they looked like people who were used to getting what they wanted, and it was only as I learned more about their case that I realised that, in this instance at least, they'd been made helpless. It was that, as much as the terror to which they'd been inflicted, that had caused them such consternation and persuaded them to contact us.

"Mr. Priest?" the man asked.

"He's upstairs," I said. "I'm Jez Hardwicke. I work with him."

"I'm Henry Carrington," he said. "And this is my wife, Eleanor. We have an appointment."

"Come in, please."

I led the way up the flight of stairs. The man hesitated as we reached the landing, glancing around the room as though judging it against some invisible standard. It was an odd arrangement, and clients often commented upon it: the two rooms were off the landing, with another flight of stairs climbing to the second floor, where Atticus's neighbour had his flat. The office kitchen, such as it was, was crammed into the space beneath the stairs, and the tiny bathroom was ahead. The place had been a bit of a mess when I had started working for Atticus, and I'd insisted that we spend some time improving it. The carpets needed to be replaced, but we had at least given them a wash; the walls needed repainting, and I'd done my best to distract from them with colourful prints by Kandinsky and Klimt and Mondrian; the ugly wooden cupboard that housed a defunct electricity meter probably ought to have been removed.

"Which way?" Henry said.

"Straight ahead," I said, indicating the open door.

Atticus was leaning against the edge of his desk as we came in. "Good morning. Mr. and Mrs. Carrington?"

"That's right," the man said, introducing himself and his wife for a second time.

"Nice to meet you both," Atticus said.

The Carringtons hesitated in the doorway as if unsure whether it had been such a good idea to have come here after all. I suspected they were used to offices that were a little sleeker and more professional, but I knew their hesitation came from Atticus, too; he had a way of unnerving people even when he was being polite. There was something about the coolness of his demeanour that gave the impression he saw right through you.

I knew he would've noted their discomfort, but doubted he'd think to say anything to try to put them at ease. That tended to be one of my main responsibilities in our professional relationship.

"Please," I said. "Come in and take a seat."

The sofa was in the bay window. It was usually covered in books and papers, but I'd tidied things up as best I could when I arrived earlier that morning. Eleanor crossed the room and sat down while Henry sat stiffly beside her, his hands clasped tightly in his lap.

"Thank you for seeing us," he said.

"My pleasure," Atticus replied. "You told me a little about your problem. I was telling Jez—it's very unusual."

"No, it's *ridiculous*," Henry corrected, "at least that's what I would've said before. It doesn't seem so foolish now. We're at the end of our tethers."

"It would be helpful if you could go through it again for Jez's benefit."

I took a notepad and pen from the desk. They exchanged a glance, and then Eleanor nodded and began.

"It's about our house," she said, her voice steady but with an undercurrent of tension. "We bought it six months ago. It's an old property near West Tytherly. You might have heard of it—Hallows House."

"I've actually visited it," I said. "The gardens are open to the public."

"They were," she replied. "That was before we bought it."

I turned to Atticus. "It's a very impressive place," I said for his benefit.

"Forty thousand square feet," Henry said with obvious pride. "We bought it as a bit of a project. It hasn't seen much TLC over the last few years, and we'd like to bring it back to how it was before."

"Wasn't it used for the Dickens adaptation at Christmas?" I said. "I think I remember reading something about it."

"*Great Expectations*," Eleanor confirmed. "They used it as Satis House—Miss Havisham's mansion. That was before our time, too. We'd like to be able to offer it as a filming location again, but that'll be after we've finished sorting things out. I'd be worried the roof would collapse at the moment."

"Go on," Atticus encouraged. "What's the problem?"

"Okay." Eleanor sighed. She closed her eyes and shook her head, as if mortified by what she was about to tell us. "We've been noticing a series of disturbances. Things we can't explain. Noises in the night. Objects moved or broken. It sounds absurd, I know. But it's as though someone—or *something*—is in the house with us."

"The house is locked every night," Henry said. "We have security cameras covering the grounds and all the main areas inside—the stairs and the corridors. There's no sign of an intruder, and yet… things still happen."

Atticus leaned forward slightly, resting his elbows on his knees. "When did it start?"

"About a month ago," Eleanor said. "We moved in six months ago, and as I said, we decided to renovate. The whole house needs work, but we thought a good place to start would be the cellar. Out of the way, easy to get to without disturbing anything else. We wanted to convert it into somewhere we could keep our wine."

"This is where you'll think we've lost our minds," Henry said ruefully. "And you'd be within your rights to think that, but we've run out of rational explanations, and this is what we're left with."

"Go on," Atticus said again.

"For years, there's been a coffin in the cellar."

"A coffin?" I said, unable to hide my surprise.

"A coffin," he repeated. "Supposedly with the body of someone called Nell Kierkegaard inside it."

"The villagers call her Black Nell," Eleanor said. "We knew about the coffin and the legend when we bought the house, but we thought it was just a bit of colour. They say that Nell was a nursemaid at the house two hundred years ago who had an illegitimate child with the owner. That would have meant immediate ostracization in those days, so she scalded it to death in the bath in what we call the Blue Room. She was caught and convicted, and they hanged her. They say her body was brought back to the house and left in the cellar, with the warning that moving her would bring disaster. There's a tiny glass window in the front of the coffin, and if you look through it, you can see part of her remains."

Atticus raised an eyebrow. "Why on earth would they bring her remains back to the house?"

Henry shrugged. "I know. The whole thing is stupid, and it doesn't make sense, but some of the locals are superstitious, and they believe it."

"Must have been spread around for another reason."

"That's what we thought," Henry said. "It looked like Nell's story came from one of the men who owned the house before us. The place has been in the Auster family for four hundred years. This man—Jack Auster—owned it in the thirties, and, from what we've found out, he was a bit of an eccentric. Loved to shock the local gentry with pranks—they called him 'Mad Jack' because of it. He owned a theatre in London and—at least this is how the story goes—he'd have people down for what he called 'spiritual weekends.' He told everyone the house was haunted, and it looked like he was able to use that to make money. There's a book written about him, and there were mentions in the newspapers at the time—correspondents who went down to visit reporting the same things that we're seeing now."

"He was involved in the theatre," I repeated. "Someone who might have had the means to make people believe things that weren't really happening?"

"Of course," Henry said. "We thought the same thing, but Jack's been dead for decades, and things are happening now."

"We know it's stupid," Eleanor said, "but we don't know what else to suggest."

Atticus was watching them both carefully. I would've expected him to dismiss their story as nonsense, but, to my surprise, he seemed to be lending it a credence I didn't think it deserved.

"So you ignored the curse and moved the remains?"

"When we started the renovations," Henry said. "It all started after that. It was nothing much at first. Strange noises, objects out of place. But then it got worse. Glasses were smashed in the kitchen. We'd hear doors opening and closing when no one else was in the house. I found our dog—and he's normally *very* calm—whimpering at the top of the cellar stairs."

"And where's the coffin now?"

"We put it back," Henry said.

"We *know* how this makes us look," Eleanor said. "We're both computer scientists. We're both *rational*. Neither of us believe in ghosts. Even talking about it this way feels preposterous."

"And yet you returned the coffin."

"We thought perhaps… well, perhaps it would stop if we put it back."

"But it hasn't," Henry said. "And Eleanor is right, we're not superstitious, but we don't feel safe in our own home anymore. And things are happening more and more frequently."

Atticus studied them for a long moment.

"Can you help us?" he asked.

"What exactly would you like me to do?"

"Find out what's happening."

Atticus paused for a moment more and then nodded. "We'll need to come and visit. Spend some time there. I'm assuming you'd have the space for us to stay overnight?"

"There are twenty-five bedrooms," Henry said. "Plenty of space."

"How about tonight?"

"As soon as that?"

"If it's convenient," Atticus said. "I don't see any reason to wait."

Henry looked over at his wife, and the two of them shared a nod. "That would be perfect. The sooner we can get to the bottom of what's happening, the better."

"Excellent." Atticus stood and extended his hand to Henry. "We'll be over this afternoon."

2

Atticus drove us out to West Tytherly in his battered old Volvo. Hallows House was at the end of a long gravel carriage drive flanked by towering yews and rolling fields that seemed to stretch endlessly under the late afternoon's slate-grey sky.

"1560," Atticus said.

"I'm sorry?"

"I did a little research," he said. "The first reference to Hallows House was in 1560. It was originally built by Neville Auster on land he bought from a dissolved monastery. It passed out of his family forty years later when he went broke but was bought back again by his son Thomas. The original property was more modest, but the owner in 1800—Richard Auster—decided to enlarge it and added two ranges, one at the back and one at the front. It's been in the Auster family for nearly five hundred years with the only breaks being when Neville lost it and then when Cromwell's men took it over during the Civil War."

"Until the last owner's financial problems."

"Correct," Atticus said. "Jameson Auster. Know how much the Carringtons had to pay to buy it?"

"Oh, I don't know." I shrugged and guessed: "Fifteen million."

"It was on the market for nineteen, and they bought it for fourteen."

"And they sold their company for three hundred million," I said. "Pocket change to them."

The road twisted around, and we passed into and then out of a shallow dell. An old chapel sat off to the side. Its stone walls had been softened by creeping ivy, and arches framed empty windows, their delicate tracery long since weathered away by time and the elements. Moss clung to the crumbling masonry, and tufts of grass sprouted between rafters where tiles had long since fallen.

I looked over at it as we passed. "Does that belong to the house?"

"Yes," he said. "Built by Neville in 1569. He was Catholic—private chapels weren't unusual then, especially when you could be sent to prison for going to Mass."

The house appeared as we turned the final corner. It wasn't just large; it was imposing and obviously designed to make an impression, a goal that it comfortably achieved. It was a grand, symmetrical mansion with a portico supported by four great columns, its pale limestone façade weathered by centuries of wind and rain. The lawn stretching out before it was a perfect emerald-green, broken only by the gravel drive that swept up to the front entrance. A smaller, neoclassical outbuilding sat at the foot of the wooded hillside behind the house.

"They built these places to be seen," Atticus said. "Status symbols first, places to live second."

I looked up at it; the huge building loomed over us. "Perfect place for a ghost story."

Atticus turned and grinned at me. "*Isn't* it?"

3

We pulled up in front of the sweeping stone steps leading to the entrance. We got out, took our overnight bags from the boot and then climbed the steps to the entrance. The front door opened before we could knock, to reveal Henry Carrington. He waved us in briskly.

"Good afternoon," he said. "How are you both?"

I could see that Atticus was already distracted, his attention passing from a quick assessment of our client to the interior of the house beyond.

"We're very well," I said for both of us.

"Thank you again for coming," he said, leading us into the vast entry hall. "I can't tell you how pleased we are to have you here."

Eleanor appeared a moment later, dressed as impeccably as before, her hands clasped tightly in front of her.

"Maeve has prepared two of the guest rooms for you," she said. "Shall I take you upstairs to leave your things?"

"Please," I said.

"This way," she said, pointing to the grand staircase. "We'll get you settled, and then perhaps you'd like to have a look around."

Atticus didn't seem to be paying attention to the conversation. "I'd like to start in the cellar," he said.

"Let's drop off our things first," I said.

He looked at me irritably, and then, perhaps realising that he was coming off as a little eccentric, he smiled. "Yes, of course. I'm getting ahead of myself. I'm just very keen to get started."

The manor's interior was a curious blend of old-world charm and modern convenience. The high ceilings and ornate mouldings suggested the long history of the place, but they clashed with the sleek, minimalist furnishings the Carringtons had introduced.

"The renovations are ongoing," Eleanor explained, catching my glance at a pile of paint cans in one corner. "It was a total mess when we took it over. We've tried to preserve the original features where we can while we bring things up to date."

Our rooms were on the first floor. We climbed the stairs, and Eleanor indicated we should go to the rear of the house. Our rooms were on either side of a sub-landing. There was a suit of armour to one side, and portraits of a series of similar-looking men had been hung side by side.

Atticus pointed. "The Austers?"

"That's right," Henry said. "The portraits came with the house. We thought it'd be nice to leave them up."

Eleanor pointed to a door. "That's you," she said to Atticus. She pointed to the door on the other side of the landing. "And that's you."

"Thank you," I said.

Atticus looked impatient to get started again. "Shall we reconvene downstairs in ten minutes?"

"Perfect," Henry said.

4

The grandeur of Hallows House was heightened by its elevated position. It provided sweeping vistas of the carefully designed parkland and then the arable fields beyond. My room was spacious and well-appointed, offering a stunning view of the gardens at the back of the house and the wooded area that clung to the flanks of the steep hill to the north.

I left my overnight bag on the bed and knocked on Atticus's door, but there was no reply. I went back downstairs and followed the sound of conversation to the enormous drawing room at the front of the house. Atticus was there already, speaking with Henry and Eleanor.

"There you are," he said. "We're just about to go down and take a look at the cellar."

We followed Henry into the hallway and then to the back of the house. It was enormous, and I found my sense of direction was quickly scrambled.

We reached the kitchen, and Henry gestured toward the set of stairs door off to the right. "Down here."

The air grew noticeably cooler as we descended the stone staircase, and smelled faintly of damp earth and sawdust.

"What's down here?" Atticus said.

"There are twenty rooms," Henry said. "Laundry, boiler room, then the rest are used for storage. Some of them flooded when the sump pump failed last year. We're in the process of drying them out. Thinking about digging some of them out and putting in a pool."

It was difficult to find my bearings, but I thought he led us towards the front of the house.

"In here."

He opened the door to what I saw was a newly installed wine cellar. The shelves lining the walls had already been stocked with wine bottles. Soft, recessed lighting cast a glow over the polished oak racks, illuminating the deep reds and crisp whites nestled in their climate-controlled home. The floor was a smooth slate, cool underfoot, and the walls were exposed brick. A state-of-the-art temperature-control panel was mounted near the entrance, and a rolling ladder was fixed to the far wall, allowing access to the highest shelves, where the rarest and most expensive vintages would be stored. A tasting table had been set up in the middle of the room: a thick slab of reclaimed wood supported by sturdy iron legs, surrounded by high-backed stools.

But the item that really caught the eye was the most incongruous: a wooden coffin, standing upright against the far wall.

"There she is," Eleanor said, her voice tight. "Black Nell."

It was a strange thing to see, especially in the newly redecorated cellar. The coffin was unassuming: rough-hewn wood, with an iron latch securing the lid. There was a small glass window in the centre, and when I stooped to look, I could just make out the curves of three rib bones.

"Bizarre," I said.

"You don't need to tell us that," Henry said.

Atticus knelt and looked at the bottom edge of the coffin. "You said you moved it?"

"We had to," Eleanor said. "Couldn't do the work in here until she was out of the way. We wanted to get rid of her completely."

Atticus ran his fingers along the edge of the coffin. "It's not as simple as just taking it to the dump."

"No," she said. "Not at all. Turns out there are all sorts of things you need to do. We had to report her to the authorities first, and then we needed a license just to move her. We spoke to a funeral director, and they said that if the remains were legitimate, we'd either have to arrange a proper burial or donate her to a museum."

"But then there's the issue of proving where the remains came from in the first place," Atticus said.

"Well, quite," Eleanor said. "We hadn't got to that when it all started happening, and then Maeve told us what happened the last time her remains were moved."

"The west wing burned down," Henry said. "And the time before that, the youngest son of the family drowned in the bath. When you hear stories like that and you have things happening in the house that you can't explain, sometimes you don't want to tempt fate."

"So you brought her back again, but the disturbances haven't stopped."

"No," he said.

"You must've *really* annoyed her."

We spent another twenty minutes in the cellar. Atticus inspected every corner, working silently and ignoring our hosts, who seemed very keen to leave. I could understand that; the space had an atmosphere to it that I found unsettling. It was difficult to put it into words, but it was more than the fact that there was a coffin with human remains propped up against the wall. The air felt unusually cold, and I felt a prickling sensation running up and down the back of my neck. I'm not superstitious, and I don't believe in the supernatural, but it was undeniable that there was an atmosphere in the cellar. It almost gave me reason to reconsider, and what would happen later would underscore that.

Atticus straightened up and dusted off his hands. "Good."

"Good?"

"I mean in the sense that I'm finished here. Perhaps we could have a look around the rest of the house."

5

We spent the next hour touring the house. Atticus was meticulous, examining every room, every door and window, asking questions that seemed unrelated to the task at hand. He ran his fingers along the edges of windowsills, knocked on walls, and noted where the floorboards creaked and where they didn't. He studied the placement of furniture and light fixtures, occasionally crouching to inspect something at skirting level or standing back to take in the broader architecture. Eleanor and Henry followed us, answering his occasional questions with a mixture of curiosity and bemusement.

As we moved through the house, I couldn't shake the feeling of being watched. I'm aware that I will invite ridicule by including that in this recounting of the case, but I can only record the way the place made me feel. Of course, I knew then—just as I know now—that it was an irrational reaction, but it clung to me all the same. Perhaps it was the weight of the legend, the knowledge that people had believed the house to be haunted for years. Or maybe it was the fact that there were supposed to be human remains in a coffin in the basement just below us and that the atmosphere down there had given me goosebumps. Either way, I found myself glancing over my shoulder more often than I liked.

"You said there are cameras," Atticus said. "Could I have a look at the feeds?"

The Carringtons led us to the billiard room on the ground floor. We sat down while Henry found a tablet in a desk at the back, waking it and navigating to the home automation app that controlled the cameras and alarms. He gave it to Atticus, and he tilted it so that I could see the screen, too. It was divided into squares, each showing footage from one of the cameras that had been installed inside and outside the house.

"I can set it so that we're notified if any of the cameras see movement," Henry said.

"The last disturbance—when was that?"

"Three nights ago," he said.

"Did any of the cameras see anything?"

"Not a thing. The doors and windows were all locked, too. No one came inside, and no one was moving around."

* * *

By the time we'd finished the tour, dusk was settling over the grounds, casting the house into shadow. The Carringtons invited us to join them for dinner. The dining room had been prepared for us; the long oak table stretched the length of the room, lit by a chandelier that looked like it had been imported from a Parisian hotel. The food was prepared by their private chef: pan-seared venison with a blackberry jus, accompanied by root vegetables that they proudly announced had been grown in the estate's walled garden. It was, by some margin, the best meal I'd had in a while.

Conversation, at first, was light. Eleanor and Henry spoke about their business: a successful medical-focused AI startup they had sold to Microsoft. Their move to the countryside, they explained, had been motivated by a desire for something real after years in the tech world. They wanted land, peace, and heritage.

"London felt… transient," Henry admitted. "You spend years building something, and when it's gone, it's like it was never there. This place has history. It has roots."

They spoke about the house and the renovations they'd done, the effort to modernise without stripping away the character. And, inevitably, the topic of the village came up.

"It's been a mixed experience," Eleanor said, choosing her words carefully. "Most people have been welcoming. But there are others…"

She trailed off, and Henry picked up the thread. "Let's just say we've made a few mistakes since we bought the house, and not everyone is prepared to give us a second chance. You come into a place like this, where the house has been in the same family for ever, and feathers get ruffled." He shrugged. "But it is what it is—we can only try to do our best."

Atticus listened, offering little in the way of opinion. I could tell he was more interested in what they weren't saying than what they were, but they didn't seem keen to rake over old coals for our benefit.

By the time the meal ended, the sky outside was black, and the house was awash in lamplight. Eleanor caught my eye as we stood to leave the table.

"I'd like to say I *hope* tonight is uneventful," she said. "But it would be good if it *wasn't*. You wonder, sometimes, whether you're going mad. It would be a relief to have someone independent to corroborate what we've been saying."

"We'll set up camp down here," Atticus said.

"Make yourselves at home," she said. "There's food and drink in the kitchen—just help yourselves."

6

I mentioned earlier that I'm not a superstitious person, but that night, when Atticus suggested we find a spot to keep watch, I was relieved when he didn't suggest the cellar. He asked my opinion, and when I suggested the billiards room—centrally placed, and within reach of all the other key rooms on the ground floor of the house—he agreed.

The Carringtons had gone to bed, and the house had settled into an eerie silence broken only by the occasional creak of the floorboards as the old building adjusted itself in the night. We sat in opposite chairs, the embers of the fireplace still glowing faintly.

"What do you think?" Atticus said.

"I think there'll be an explanation for whatever is happening."

"Don't believe in ghosts?"

I stared at him. "Of course I don't." I saw his quizzical expression. "Don't tell me you *do*."

"There are things that can't always be easily explained," he said.

"I know. But… ghosts?"

He shrugged and then gave me a wink. "We'll soon see, won't we?"

* * *

It was a little after midnight when I heard it.

A scraping sound, as if something was being dragged.

Atticus met my gaze. He had heard it too.

The sound continued, low and deliberate, like something being pushed across the floor. It wasn't the erratic settling of the house; it was controlled and intentional.

Atticus put his finger to his lips and then pointed to the door. We rose in unison, moving as stealthily as we could.

I could hear the noise more clearly now. It sounded as if it was coming from the kitchen.

Atticus motioned for me to follow, and we crept into the hallway. The wooden floor beneath us creaked, and, just as I put my weight on a particularly noisy board and froze, there came a deafening crash.

We rushed to the kitchen. I switched on my phone's flashlight and flicked the beam across the room.

There was nothing.

No one.

Atticus frowned, taking a step forward.

A large kitchen island dominated the space, its marble countertop gleaming in the light of our torches. As we edged around it, we saw shards of porcelain scattered across the tiles.

I rounded the island and saw what had happened.

The stack of plates that I remembered seeing on our tour was on the floor. They had smashed into a thousand fragments. A cafetière, too, had been dashed to pieces.

Atticus crouched over the debris.

Then, from behind us, coming from somewhere upstairs, there came a second loud crash: the unmistakable sound of breaking glass.

I spun around so fast I almost tripped over my own feet. I rushed back to the corridor that connected the main body of the house to the grange, with Atticus close behind me. We reached the stairs and sprinted up, taking the treads two at a time.

We reached the long corridor with the doors to our rooms, they were closed, so we continued around into the rear grange. The door to the first bedroom we reached was ajar. We'd been inside as a part of our tour, although now—of course—I couldn't find the light switch and had to rely on my phone's flashlight.

The wall had heavy oak panels, while a large bed and an antique chaises longue took up most of the space. There was an enormous Inglenook fireplace to my right; huge, the kind of thing you could practically stand inside, its heavy stone surround blackened with the residue of centuries of fires. A solid oak mantel stretched across its width, and the deep recess of the hearth was large enough to accommodate an entire armchair if someone had the inclination.

I swung the light to the left and found the source of the crash.

A large vase that had been on a bedside table lay shattered on the floor, slivers of porcelain and flowers scattered across the wooden boards.

* * *

The Carringtons arrived as we were clearing up the mess from the broken vase.

"*See*," Henry said. "We *told* you."

"You did," Atticus said.

Eleanor was pale. "I heard another crash."

"That was from the kitchen. A stack of plates was pushed onto the floor. I think it's safe to say that it wasn't an accident. Someone would've had to give them a hefty shove."

"Someone?" She shook her head. "No. Some*thing*."

"I don't know about that," Atticus said. "There'll be an explanation for what's been happening."

"Really?" Henry said. "What? Because that's what we thought, but it keeps happening, and we can't think of anything to explain it. The cameras ping me if they see something, and they didn't. The only thing left—the *only* thing—is that it's because we moved that damned coffin."

They were both frightened, and I could understand why. The last fifteen minutes had been disconcerting, and it was difficult to understand Atticus's confidence that there was a sensible explanation for what was going on.

7

We retired to bed after that, and, to my surprise, I found I was able to manage a few hours of sleep. The excitement meant I'd forgotten to close the curtains, so I woke at six with the dawn's light streaming in. Everything seemed very different now, and it took a moment to recall the confusion of just a few hours earlier. I got up, took a long shower and got dressed. I was just lacing up my shoes when there was a knock at the door. I tried to open it before remembering I'd locked it.

Atticus was outside. "Scared?"

"No," I said indignantly.

"You locked the door."

"Force of habit."

"Black Nell wouldn't be stopped by a locked door, though, would she? She'd float right through."

He gave me a big, stagecy wink, and I immediately felt like a fool. It was fair enough, the whole thing felt ridiculous in the cold light of day, but it had been very different last night.

And the fact remained: what had happened was still completely inexplicable.

"Want some breakfast?" he said.

"I'm starving."

"You need to fill up—we're going to be busy today."

* * *

Atticus and I found our way downstairs, following the smell of coffee and something warm and slightly sweet. The gloom in the dining room had been banished by the sun pouring through the high sash windows, and the oppressive stillness that had pressed in on us during the night was gone, replaced by the ordinary sounds of a waking household: footsteps moving along corridors, the faint hum of a vacuum cleaner, the distant clatter of pots in the kitchen.

The Carringtons' cook, a woman in a crisp white chef's coat, came through from the kitchen, wiping her hands on a towel.

"Good morning," she said, her accent betraying her local origins.

"Good morning," Atticus said. "I'm Atticus, and this is Jez."

She smiled down at us both. "I'm Lorna. Sorry if you've been waiting. Lots of distractions this morning. Had a lot to clear up."

"Yes," Atticus said. "From last night—the plates."

"What a bloody mess—excuse my French."

Atticus eyed her carefully. "What do you think happened?"

Lorna snorted. "What do I think happened? Isn't it obvious? Someone knocked them over. Whether it was carelessness or something else, I couldn't say."

"You don't believe it was anything unnatural?"

"Black Nell?" She laughed. "*Please.* I've worked here long enough not to be spooked by a bit of a rattle in the night.

People hear what they want to hear, especially in a house like this. I've worked in country houses my whole career, and they all have their oddities."

"But the Carringtons are convinced," I pointed out.

"Nothing against them, but they're city folk. Used to walls that don't settle and old beams that don't groan. I don't blame them, but they get a few things they can't explain and suddenly they're living in a ghost story." She clapped her hands together. "Now then—enough of all that foolishness. What can I get you gentlemen for breakfast?"

"I'll have some porridge, please. With honey, if you've got it."

She nodded, looking at me.

"Same," I said.

She made her way to the kitchen.

Atticus wandered over to the windows and gazed out across the grounds. "What do you think happened last night? After sleeping on it, I mean."

"I have no idea what to think," I said. "As far as we can make out, the only people inside the house were us and the Carringtons, and they were upstairs in bed. They've checked the cameras—both inside *and* outside—and they don't show anything. And things that *shouldn't* have fallen to the floor definitely *did*."

He steepled his hands, his fingers touching. "Interesting, isn't it?"

"Do you know what happened?"

He pursed his lips. "Not exactly. I have a couple of ideas, but I'm not quite there—not yet, anyway."

Lorna returned, setting two bowls of steaming porridge and mugs of coffee in front of us.

Atticus took a spoonful of his porridge, and I followed suit. I was halfway through my bowl when Eleanor Carrington appeared in the doorway.

She looked tired. Dark circles sat under her eyes, and her normally sleek hair was loose and a little ruffled around her shoulders.

"Good morning," she said. "Did you sleep?"

"Very well," Atticus said.

"How did you manage that? I think I must've had an hour, and it might've been less."

"I find sleep comes easier when I've been thinking about something," he said, taking another spoonful of porridge. "And last night gave me plenty to think about."

Eleanor sighed, pulling a chair out and sitting opposite us. "And? Do you have any thoughts?"

"A few," he said. "I'd like to speak to the staff, if that's all right."

She nodded. "Of course. Who do you want to start with?"

"We spoke with Lorna," he said.

"What did she think?"

"That there's a rational explanation for it."

"She probably thinks I've lost my marbles."

"I saw there were cottages on the estate," Atticus continued. "Does anyone live in those?"

"No," she said. "We use them as accommodation for our shooting weekends. They're empty most of the time."

"You said you have a housekeeper?"

"Yes—Maeve."

"And does she live nearby?"

"West Tytherly."

"Who else is here regularly?"

"Maeve's husband is head gardener, and we have two full-time gardeners who work with him. Mary cleans for us—she comes in every day. And Henry's PA works from the office in the old bothy."

"That's it?" Atticus asked.

"Yes," she said. "No one else lives in the house—it's just us."

Atticus stirred his porridge. "Thank you. If you could ask Maeve to come and find us, that would be very helpful."

"She'll be here in an hour," Eleanor said. "I'll tell her. Do you have somewhere to work? I was thinking maybe you could use the library."

"That would be perfect," he said.

Atticus finished the last of his porridge, and I followed suit, and as Eleanor excused herself, Atticus turned to me.

"I've got a couple of things I want to look at."

"Want me to come with you?"

"No," he said. "It's fine. I'll be back in an hour to see Maeve. We can do that together."

8

I had an hour to kill and decided to take Eleanor's advice and retreat to the library and do a little research. The Carringtons had emailed me with a list of the websites they'd found during their research into the history of Hallows House and, in particular, the story of Black Nell. They'd been told about the legend by locals in the village and said that, even though they thought it ridiculous, in the absence of any other explanation for what had been happening, they'd been unable to stop themselves from going down the rabbit hole.

I opened my laptop and did the same.

It soon became obvious that Black Nell—or Nell Kierkegaard, to give her her full name—was a staple of local folklore. The story was luridly interesting, but, as I dug a little deeper, some rather significant cracks in the story started to appear.

Firstly, the name: Nell Kierkegaard sounded plausible enough until I visited the genealogical website I used for my research and found the surname 'Kierkegaard' was non-existent in Hampshire during the early 1800s. The etymology was most likely Danish, I thought, and I couldn't find a single Kierkegaard in the entire county.

It wasn't an auspicious start, and it didn't get any better.

I visited the website of the National Archive and then a site that listed every execution in the United Kingdom from the eighteenth century onward. There was no record of a Nell Kierkegaard—or *any* Kierkegaard—ever being executed.

I changed tack and looked into the recent history of Hallows House. As Atticus had already found out, the estate had been in the Auster family for nearly five hundred years. The Austers had made their fortune through wool trading in the late Middle Ages, capitalising on the booming textile industry that once made Hampshire one of the wealthiest counties in England. The property had been passed down through the generations, each successive heir leaving their mark: expanding the grounds, modernising the interiors, or adding their own eccentric flourishes.

The last owner—Jameson Auster—had inherited the house from his father in the late 1990s. Unlike his ancestors, Jameson had little interest in maintaining the estate's grandeur and saw it instead as an asset to leverage. He secured a large loan on the property to fund his ambitious business ventures in high-end hospitality, planning to turn the house into an exclusive country retreat. The venture, however, was short-lived. Mismanagement and mounting debts led to the collapse of his company, and the bank came calling. Jameson was forced to sell the house to cover his debts, and it passed out of the Auster family. The Carringtons swooped in with their considerable wealth and snapped it up at auction.

Jameson had managed to find enough money after paying his creditors to purchase the local pub and had moved there.

His social media was toxic, and he made no secret of his resentment towards his successors. I also found a report on the website of the Salisbury *Journal* saying that the Carringtons had sued him for trespass after he'd repeatedly been seen wandering the estate grounds as if trying to reclaim what had once been his.

I thought Atticus would want to speak to him.

As I pieced together the timeline, I found something else that was intriguing: the sale of the house coincided with Black Nell's appearance on two websites dedicated to the weird and the wonderful. The legend of the curse had never been reported online before, and the sudden publication just after the Carringtons moved in was, at best, a little suspicious.

I closed my laptop and went to the window, where, to my surprise, I saw Atticus walking across the lawn from the direction of the old chapel. He had his hands in the pockets of his leather jacket, and his head was down, most likely listening to something on the earphones he'd pressed into his ears. A car came down the drive and overtook him, and, as it pulled up, I saw it was driven by a woman in her late fifties or early sixties. I looked at my watch and saw that an hour had passed; it must have been Maeve arriving for work.

I slid my computer back into my bag and went to meet Atticus at the door.

9

Eleanor told Maeve that we wanted to speak to her, and she joined me and Atticus in the library. I would have said she was in her late fifties and was sturdily built, with the kind of posture that suggested a lifetime of hard work. Her salt-and-pepper hair was pulled back into a neat bun, though a few loose strands framed her face. She had a friendly face: a ready smile and a sparkle in her eyes, the kind that made her seem warm and approachable.

"You want to speak to me about what's been happening?" she said as she sat down.

"Yes, please," Atticus said.

"Heard you saw her last night."

"Saw her?"

"Nell."

"No. Not exactly."

"But she smashed the plates in the kitchen and the vase upstairs?"

"*Someone* did," Atticus said. "Why'd you think it was Nell?"

"Because who *else* could it have been? You know I've seen her before?"

"Really?"

She nodded. "There's a bridge over the road between Hallows House and Norman House. I used to live here with my mum and dad, back when Mr. Auster was in charge. There was one night, must have been around this time of year, pretty late, I was eighteen or nineteen, and I was coming back from West Tytherly. I came under that bridge, and I swear to God I saw a body dressed in black hanging from the bridge. I stopped and turned back, and, although she was gone, I'm telling you now, there was someone or something watching me." She folded her arms across her chest. "So—when we get someone coming in here already convinced that it *couldn't* be her, that it has to be something you can explain, then I'd say to them—how do you explain what's happening now, and how do you explain what I saw?"

"What were you doing late at night in West Tytherly?"

"I was at the Black Horse," she said, before realising that Atticus had asked her the question while knowing the answer. She smiled and then laughed. "No, no, no—I swear I wasn't pissed!"

Atticus chuckled. "I'm not saying you were. And I'm not doubting strange things are happening here—and *have* happened. They have. I'm going to do my best to explain them." He paused. "Can I ask how long you've worked here?"

"At Hallows?" She glanced away and rubbed a hand against her forehead. "Over twenty years. Might be twenty-five, now I come to think of it."

"You worked for the previous owner, then? Mr. Auster."

"Jameson? I did. And his father. And my mother worked for his father's father."

"That'd be 'Mad Jack'—right?"

"He was certainly a character."

"The Barretts have been very loyal to the Austers, then."

"They were always good to us."

"And it was a shame to see them leave?"

"It was. Shame for the house, too. You know it's been in the family ever since it was built?"

"That's right. It's remarkable."

"The *history* of it... I always liked thinking that I was working for the family who built the house."

"But the Carringtons still kept you on."

"They did," she said with a smile. "And I'm very grateful to them."

"Did they keep anyone else on who worked for Mr. Auster?"

She nodded. "Everyone who wanted to stay could stay. Mary cleans on Mondays, Wednesdays and Fridays. My husband, Clive, is the head gardener. There are three of them—Clive plus Steve and Matt. And then there are the contractors who worked on the house as and when they were needed. It's a team—they were asked if they wanted to stay to work on the renovation."

"And did they?"

"Everyone except Graham."

"And who's he?"

"Painter and decorator. He had a falling-out with Mr. Carrington and said he wouldn't work for him."

"A falling-out over what?"

"The work that he did. I don't know all the ins and outs, but, from what I heard, Mr. Carrington said Graham hadn't done a job professionally enough, and he wasn't going to pay the invoice. They had a right old set-to about it—I heard the two of them shouting at each other before Graham drove off. Haven't seen him since."

Atticus looked at me. "We'd better have a word with him." He turned back to Maeve. "Do you have his details?"

"I don't, but I know where he'll be—he has his breakfast in the Black Horse every morning."

"The pub Jameson Auster bought after he left here?"

"That's right—the two of them have been friends for years. Graham's father worked for Mr. Auster's father."

Atticus nodded.

She looked at him and then at me. "Have you been down the cellar?"

"We have."

"What did you think?"

"It has an *atmosphere*."

"I've always felt like there's someone watching me. That prickly feeling on the back of the neck… that's what I always have. And there was one time, a year or two after I started working here, when I was cleaning down there… I heard footsteps, and then the door closed on me. And I swear no one else was there."

"So *you* wouldn't have moved the coffin?"

"Not a chance," she said. "Mr. and Mrs. Carrington told me they were going to move it for their wine cellar, and I wanted to tell them about the legend, but it felt so stupid and childish that I didn't. And then whatever has been happening started to happen and…" She paused. "Well, obviously you've been asked to come here and work it all out. Good luck, that's all I'll say. I'll be pleased when it's quiet again."

10

Atticus decided that he wanted to speak to Graham Gorman, the disgruntled decorator who had argued with Henry Carrington. I found his number online and called him to see if we could meet. Maeve had been right: he *was* in the Black Horse in West Tytherly and said he was happy to wait for us. We arrived and parked next to a van stencilled with the name of Gorman's business.

Atticus rolled his eyes. "Strokes of Genius."

"I quite like it," I said, shutting the passenger-side door and following him inside.

There were two people sitting at a table near the bar: the man wearing paint-splattered overalls was evidently Gorman, and the other, his trousers stained with mud and with a pointer asleep at his feet, looked as if he might have just finished a walk. There were two pints of ale on the table.

"Hello," I said, approaching the man in the overalls.

"Jez?"

"That's right—and this is my colleague, Atticus."

"Graham Gorman," the man said, offering his hand; we both shook it.

"Thanks for seeing us," Atticus said.

"This is about the Carringtons?"

"That's right," he said.

The other man chuckled and shook his head. "Awful people."

Atticus glanced over at him. "Excuse me?"

"Absolutely *awful*, both of them."

"I'm sorry," I said, "who are you?"

"Jameson Auster."

"Ah," Atticus said. "You owned the house before them."

"I did."

"And you bought this pub after you moved out."

He nodded. "A little smaller than the house, but at least it isn't haunted."

I paid him a little more attention. He was a broad-shouldered man in his early fifties, with weathered skin that suggested time spent outdoors. His hair was clipped short, and he had the air of someone who had once been used to getting his way but was irritated to find he'd since been forced to make compromises.

"Have you met them yet?" Auster asked us.

"We have," Atticus said.

"Made quite an impact in the village since they arrived—right, Graham?"

Gorman let out a low chuckle and nodded. "That's one way of putting it."

Atticus pulled up a chair. "How do you mean?"

Auster leaned back, stretching his legs. "They come here flashing their money, buy up the estate like it's bloody Monopoly, and then immediately start changing *everything*.

Bear in mind Hallows House has been here for five hundred years, and there's centuries' worth of custom that've grown up around it. They don't care about any of that—the house *or* the village—they don't care about anyone but themselves."

"Changing things how?" I asked.

"This'll sound petty, but it really isn't. They've cut off the old permissive footpath that ran through their estate."

"It's not petty," Gorman said.

"People around here have walked that path for generations, but now it's all locked gates and 'private property' signs. I always used to let people walk there if they wanted to. My family never made a fuss about it."

"I walked the dog there every morning," Gorman said. "Now we have to go the long way round."

Atticus folded his arms. "So there's resentment here?"

Auster nodded. "You could say that."

"And would it be fair to say you're not a fan?"

"You know they sued me for trespass, don't you?" He shrugged. "Bloody *trespass*. I heard they'd closed the path, and I wasn't having it—made it a point to use it, just to show solidarity. Letter from their solicitors the next day. But that sums them up, doesn't it? Petty, nasty, awful people."

Gorman joined in with the communal kicking. "Did you hear about the spa they want to build?"

Atticus said he hadn't.

Gorman snorted, shaking his head. "Of course you haven't. They've kept it quiet—at least as quiet as they can. But the plans are in with the council now, and it's caused a bloody uproar."

"What are they proposing?"

"A *spa*," Gorman said darkly, swirling the dregs of his pint. "Not just any spa, mind you. A 'luxury retreat'. Full-on wellness centre—'wellness', I bloody *hate* that word—complete with a massive pool, a sauna, treatment rooms, and God knows what else. They're planning to convert one of the old barns, but it doesn't stop there. They want new access roads, more parking, and accommodation for their London guests."

"They're calling it an 'eco-retreat'," Auster added, voice dripping with sarcasm. "Like sticking a few solar panels on it makes it good for the environment. It's a monstrosity. They say it'll bring jobs and money into the village, but what they really mean is they want to cash in on city types who'll pay a fortune to sit in a hot tub and drink green juice."

Atticus glanced between them. "And the villagers aren't happy?"

Auster gave a dry laugh. "Parish council is up in arms. The planning committee's been flooded with objections. The traffic alone will be a nightmare. That road isn't built for the kind of volume they're expecting. Not to mention the noise—imagine hen parties and corporate retreats getting smashed every weekend. It'll change the village completely. This place is quiet, and people moved here to get away from all that."

Gorman nodded. "And that's before you get to the impact on the land itself. They want to run a new drainage system through part of the old meadow, where it floods in winter. It'll cause a mess. And don't even get me started on the shooting weekends."

Atticus frowned. "What about them?"

"They've ramped those up too. They're inviting corporate groups—big-money types who've never held a gun before, giving them a weekend of drinking and shooting anything that moves. The conservationists are livid. We've got red kites nesting out there, and barn owls. The noise alone will drive them away. They think they can throw money at anything and do whatever they want."

"And what about you?" Atticus asked him. "What happened with Henry Carrington? Maeve said you had a run-in."

Gorman's jaw tightened. He took a slow sip of his pint before answering, "I did some work for them. We agreed a price up front and then, halfway through, Carrington starts picking fault with the job—says it's not up to his standards, starts finding excuses not to pay." He snorted with derision. "Bastard short-changed me. Paid me barely half of what we agreed. Said if I didn't like it, I could take him to court. Not worth the hassle, and it would've been hard to prove—it would've been my word against his, and he would've had some smarmy lawyer working for him, wouldn't he, make me look like I'm lying. It still sticks in my throat. He's got millions, and he's arguing over a few grand that'd make a real difference to me like it's coming out of his last fiver."

Auster eyed us both. "You're working for him because of Black Nell?"

"That's right."

They both laughed.

"You never noticed anything when you were there?"

"Course not. You know it was my great-grandad who started all that?"

"That's what I read," I said. "Jack."

"'Mad Jack.'" He laughed again. "He was a bit of a character. No one knows for sure, but my dad said Jack bought Nell from a medical school and put her in that box to put the shit up his theatre friends."

"You don't believe the legend, then?"

"Ghosts? Come on. Course not."

I noticed Gorman hesitate; Atticus noticed, too. "You don't agree?"

Auster gave Gorman a playful punch on the shoulder. "He's superstitious, this one—always has been. Don't walk under your ladder when you've got it up, do you, Graham?"

"No, I do not," Gorman said, obviously embarrassed.

"You think there's something in it?"

"Do I believe in the supernatural?" Gorman exhaled. "I don't know. But I'm not arrogant enough to think that there might be things in this world that we don't understand. And I know, from my own personal experience in that house, things happened to me there that don't make sense. There was one time, last year, I was working down in the cellar, putting in the new racks they had made for their wine. Nell was gone—they'd moved her out. All I can say is that it suddenly went from being warm to bloody cold and that the lights cut out. And then, after I went upstairs to see if something had tripped the fuse board, my brushes had been rearranged."

"Want to know what I think happened?" Auster said with a grin. "Graham had had a couple of these"—he tapped a finger against the empty pint glass—"and forgot where he'd put his stuff."

Gorman chuckled. "Piss off."

Atticus stood. "Thanks for your time."

"Pleasure," Auster said. "I'd say I hope you find the ghost, but I think I'd prefer it if it scared them away."

11

Maeve had given us the number for Mary Wills, the house cleaner, and Atticus arranged to meet her at Pump House Bakes in nearby West Winterslow after lunch. It was a small place, squeezed into the old pump house, the kind of establishment where the same five locals sat nursing cups of tea for hours, exchanging the day's gossip with knowing looks over the rims of their mugs.

We spotted Mary immediately. She was in her late sixties, dressed in a neat navy cardigan and a pair of slacks, with wiry grey hair that had been pinned back in a tight bun. She had the kind of face that looked naturally disapproving, with deep frown lines around her mouth and sharp eyes that tracked us as we approached her table.

"Mary?" Atticus said, taking a seat opposite her.

"That's me," she replied, glancing between us. "You're the private detective, then? And you're his…" Her eyes settled on me, assessing. "Assistant?"

"Something like that," I said.

She snorted and folded her arms. "Well, I don't know what I can tell you, but Maeve said you had some questions."

Atticus leaned back in his chair. "You've worked at Hallows House for a long time?"

"Thirty-six years," she said, a note of pride in her voice. "Worked for Mr. Auster's father before him. Used to be a proper house back then. Not like it is now."

"You're not fond of the Carringtons, then?"

Mary sniffed. "Fond of them? Honestly?"

"Yes, please."

"Not really. But I don't have to like them to do my job. I keep my mouth shut, do the cleaning, and get on with it. That's what I've always done."

Atticus tilted his head. "But you don't approve of them?"

"They've no respect for the house," she said bitterly. "It's all about the money with them—fancy kitchens, posh furniture, all style and no substance. And don't get me started on what they did to poor Mr. Auster. He belonged there. His family had lived in that house for *generations*." She shook her head and pressed her lips together. "It's not right. That house should never have left the family. It wasn't meant for them."

I glanced at Atticus; his face was impassive. "And what do you think about what's been happening?"

Mary hesitated. "It's not for me to say."

"But you have an opinion?"

She let out a breath. "You're not going to laugh?"

"Not at all."

"I think it's her."

"Her?" I asked, already knowing what was coming.

"Nell," Mary said. "I know what people say—that she's just a story, that Mr. Auster's granddad made her up for a bit of fun. But I never believed that. We always knew better."

"Knew better how?" Atticus asked.

Mary leaned in. "There were *things*. Even before the Carringtons came. Little things, mind—doors that wouldn't stay locked, cold spots in rooms that should've been warm. Sometimes I'd hear footsteps upstairs when I knew the house was empty. And then they went and *moved* her." She shook her head, as if that alone explained everything.

"Then they moved her back," I pointed out.

"Too late," Mary said. "They disturbed her; now she's punishing them."

Atticus studied her. "You think a ghost is doing this?"

Mary met his gaze, unflinching. "You can believe what you like, Mr. Priest. I know what I know."

"Do you ever see Mr. Auster after he lost the house?" Atticus asked.

"In the pub," she said with a nod.

"And do you think he might be angry enough to want to scare them out?"

Mary's eyes flashed. "Mr. Auster wouldn't do that."

"But he *did* trespass," I said. "We heard about the court case."

She pursed her lips. "That was different. He had every right to be there."

"Even if the law didn't agree?"

Mary straightened in her chair. "He wouldn't have done anything like what's happening. It's Nell, I tell you. They shouldn't have touched her."

Atticus sighed and tapped his fingers on the table. "And you?" he said. "Do you wish the Carringtons would leave?"

Mary hesitated just long enough for us to notice. "I mind my own business," she said eventually. "It's not for me to say."

Atticus nodded as if she'd just confirmed something for him. "Thank you for your time. You've been very helpful."

She stood, collecting her handbag. "Just be careful," she said, giving him a pointed look. "Not everything can be explained away."

12

We spent the afternoon in Salisbury attending to other files, and then drove back to the house for a second night.

"I'm going to leave you to it," Atticus said. "I have something I'd like to test."

"What do you want me to do?"

"The same as last night," he said. "And when there's a disturbance, I want you to text me to let me know."

"There'll be another one? Tonight?"

"Oh yes," he said. "I'm sure of it. I think our being here practically guarantees it. It's one thing to frighten the Carringtons, but we've been brought here on the basis that we're rational. If *we* can't suggest a logical explanation, then, I think, the Carringtons will decide the only explanation is that the curse is true. And then they might very well decide to sell up and go."

"But the curse *isn't* true?"

He eyed me as if I'd said something stupid. "Of course it isn't," he said. "I have a good idea what's happening, but I'd like to be sure before I tell anyone else."

"Even me?"

"*Especially* you. Can't have you thinking I'm fallible, can we?"

13

I had dinner with Eleanor and Henry and then a glass of whiskey with them both in the billiards room. They asked where Atticus was, and I bluffed that he was looking into something that would help explain what had been happening. Henry asked me to elaborate, but I told him that Atticus would do that when he was confident in his conclusions; Henry didn't look satisfied with my answer, but didn't push me for anything else.

The two of them went to bed soon after that and left me downstairs, settled into an armchair with a mug of tea growing cold in my hands.

The first hour passed uneventfully. I spent most of it flipping through an old magazine I'd found on the coffee table, its pages filled with articles about shooting weekends and country retreats for rich Londoners; the sort of things that seemed to have caused the villagers to turn against the Carringtons.

The second hour was similarly quiet. I took out my laptop and turned my attention to the controversy surrounding our clients. A quick search of the local council's planning portal brought up the formal objections to the spa development.

The list of complaints was extensive: concerns over traffic, environmental damage, noise pollution. The objections couldn't be anonymous, and I recognised a few names, including Graham Gorman, and, of course, Jameson Auster.

Atticus texted me at just after one in the morning.

Be ready. There will be a disturbance in the next fifteen minutes.

I stared at the screen. I wanted to ask him how he could possibly say that, but knew he wouldn't tell me. Instead, I asked him what he wanted me to do.

Wait five minutes after it happens and then come to the boiler room in the cellar.

His timing was almost perfect.

Seven minutes had passed when there was a sound from somewhere nearby. A faint thud at first, like something being shifted or dropped.

The house had been still until now, and the noise sent a shiver through me.

I held my breath, listening.

Then: *crash*.

A sharp and sudden shattering, the unmistakable sound of glass breaking.

I stood, my heart hammering. It had come from somewhere in the house, but from where? The house was deathly silent again, as if waiting to see what I would do next.

It sounded as if it had come from upstairs.

I grabbed my phone and switched on the flashlight, moving quickly through the hall. My footsteps sounded thunderous on the wooden floor. I climbed the grand staircase, passing through the gaze of one of the Carringtons' new security cameras, and hurried around to the grange.

I reached the bedroom where the vase had smashed. Everything was as it should be.

I went to the next bedroom and saw what had happened.

Another vase was on the floor, blooms scattered amongst the shards of glass.

I heard another sound.

Downstairs.

The faint scrape of something shifting, and then another crash.

I rushed back down the stairs and turned towards the dining room.

My pulse was a drumbeat in my ears as I pushed open the door.

I swung the flashlight beam across the space. At first, everything seemed untouched: the long table, the chairs, the grand cabinet against the far wall.

But then my eyes landed on the floor near the fireplace.

The crystal decanter that had held the whisky now lay shattered on the rug, its contents soaking into the fabric, the smell of the alcohol heavy in the air.

I moved closer, stepping carefully around the shards of glass. The decanter had been on the sideboard the last time I'd seen it.

A breath of cold air brushed the back of my neck, and I turned sharply, half expecting to see someone standing behind me.

But there was no one.

My skin prickled.

Someone *had* been in here.

And then, as if to confirm it, a creak came from the hallway.

I swung my phone's flashlight toward the doorway.

It was Henry Carrington.

His face was pale. "Again?"

I was about to respond when my phone rang.

"Jez," Atticus said, "get down here."

14

I raced to the stairs, with Henry close behind me, taking them two at a time down to the cellar. The cold air hit me as I reached the bottom, and the walls seemed to close in.

Atticus was waiting in the corridor that led off from the stairs to the rooms on the north side of the cellar.

"This way," he said.

I expected him to lead us to the wine cellar and the coffin, but he didn't. Instead, he turned right, guiding us toward one of the storerooms.

"What's going on?" Henry asked, his voice sharp with impatience.

Atticus glanced at him. "You're not dressed for this," he said, gesturing at Henry's dressing gown and slippers. "It's better you stay here. By the time we get back, I'll be able to explain exactly what's been happening and who's responsible for it."

Henry looked ready to argue, his jaw tightening, but Atticus turned away before he could say anything. He pushed open the door to the storeroom and stepped inside. I followed, with Henry hesitating just beyond the threshold.

I hadn't been in this room before. It smelled of damp wood and dust. Shelves lined the walls, stacked with boxes, and a collection of old furniture was pushed up against the walls. A single bare bulb dangled from the ceiling, casting weak, flickering light. At first glance, it looked like nothing special.

But Atticus wasn't interested in the shelves or the boxes.

He crossed to the far wall and ran his fingers along the underside of a thick wooden beam that stretched down from the ceiling. His fingertips skimmed over the surface, searching, until they found a slight indentation.

"Here," he murmured.

He pressed firmly, and I heard the faintest *click*. He pushed at the top of the beam, and the bottom end swung up with a deep, reluctant creak. The top of the beam was on a hidden pivot and, now that it had been raised, it revealed a dark recess behind it.

I stepped closer and saw it wasn't just a recess: it was the yawning mouth of a tunnel. The entrance was narrow—just the width of the beam—and it would be a tight squeeze to get through. A wave of cold air rolled out, thick with the scent of earth and damp stone.

Henry gaped at him. "You knew this was here?"

"I suspected it," he said, pulling two torches from his coat pocket. He handed one of the torches to me. "You'll need this. It's a reasonable walk."

We both switched on the lights and shone them into the tunnel. A narrow, uneven passage stretched ahead, disappearing into blackness.

I glanced back at Henry, who had taken a step forward, eyes wide with disbelief.

"I can't believe this. How long has that been there?"

"I should imagine almost as long as the house," Atticus said. "I'll explain when we get back."

Henry opened his mouth, then closed it again.

I supported the beam on the pivot so Atticus could go through, and then slid inside myself, lowering it behind us. The darkness closed in and would have been complete were it not for the flashlights. The floor was uneven, with patches of damp earth. The walls had been reinforced with brick. Every step echoed in the confined space, the sound bouncing unnervingly back at us. We moved carefully, the beams of our torches cutting through the darkness.

The tunnel was dead straight. The farther into it we went, the more my unease grew. The walls dripped with moisture, with the occasional down-thrusting root jutting from the ceiling. My torch caught something on the ground ahead: fresh footprints, pressed into the damp earth.

We continued on, the passage narrowing until we had to stoop. The tunnel began to slope gently upward, and the air changed; it was fresher now.

There was a wooden trapdoor above us.

15

Atticus pushed the trapdoor. It creaked as he shouldered it open, and we clambered up and out into what I quickly realised was the abandoned chapel on the estate grounds. It was a bitterly cold night, and as we stepped out of the tunnel, I could see my breath hanging in the air. The chapel looked worse from the inside, and I could see now that it was barely standing: the walls were pitted and cracked, and the roof was missing in jagged sections, allowing the sky to spill through. We were in what had once been the vestry: a small annex to the main chapel, where priests would have robed themselves for service. I looked around and saw the flashing blue and red lights of a police car shining through the empty windows.

Atticus switched off his torch. I did the same, my breath catching as we left the chapel through a hole where the wall had collapsed, and stepped out onto the damp grass.

Four figures stood in the glow of the police car's lights.

A uniformed officer turned as we approached.

"Atticus?" he called.

"It's me," Atticus said. "Thanks for coming, Bob."

I recognised the man: it was PC Bob Carver, from Bourne Hill. I didn't recognise the other officer. I knew that Atticus and Carver had had their disagreements in the past, but it seemed they had buried the hatchet.

I looked at the man and woman who had been detained. They were standing in front of the car, and its headlights cast them in silhouette so deep I couldn't make out anything beyond their shadows.

"This is Maeve Barrett," Atticus said to the officers. "And this is her husband, Clive. They both work at the house."

I stepped away from the light so I could see them properly. Maeve's face was pale but defiant; her husband glowered with barely suppressed fury.

"We caught them coming out," Carver said. "Just like you said."

Atticus took out his phone. "I have footage of them inside the house."

"What?" Maeve said. "No, you don't."

"I followed you inside. You had a chat with your husband in the cellar. I was behind you, in the tunnel."

"So what?" Maeve said. "We haven't done anything. It was all just a joke."

"That's right," Clive said. "At worst it's trespassing, and that's not criminal, is it, officer? It's civil."

"It's aggravated trespass if you went in with intent to commit an offence," Carver said.

"And you *did* commit an offence," Atticus added. "Several, actually. Criminal damage will be easy to prove, and that's without even thinking about public mischief, intimidation under the Protection from Harassment Act, burglary."

"Burglary? We didn't take anything."

"You don't have to," Carver said. "Leaving fake evidence might be enough."

"There's fraud, too," Atticus said. "If you manipulated the situation for financial gain—for example, devaluing the property so Mr. Auster can buy it back cheaply—you'd be looking at fraud by false representation. He'd be looking at that, too."

"You can do time for that," Carver said.

Maeve glared at Carver, then back to Atticus. "You don't know what you're talking about."

"No," Atticus said. "I do. You were trying to drive them out. Both of you. You wanted them to leave, to scare them into selling so it could go back to the 'rightful' owner."

She didn't answer.

"How much did he offer to pay you?"

"This is ridiculous," she muttered.

Clive fidgeted, moving his weight from one foot to the other.

Atticus noticed. "Mr. Barrett?"

"Fifty grand," he said.

"Clive!" Maeve said. "Shut up."

"We're done," he said. "And if *we're* done, *he's* done, too." He turned to Carver. "If we help you out, does that mean you'll go easy on us?"

"I think we need to have this chat down at the station," Carver said.

He read them their rights, and, satisfied that everything was in order, he put them in the car.

Carver gestured toward the big house, several of the downstairs windows now lit. "You'll have a word with the owners?"

"We will," Atticus said. "I think they'll be very interested to hear what's been going on."

Atticus and I stood in silence for a moment, watching as the officers got into the car with the Barretts in the back and drove away.

Atticus turned to me. "Well," he said with a chuckle, "*that* was dramatic."

I let out a dry laugh, rubbing a hand over my face. "How did you know?"

Atticus straightened his coat and glanced toward the house in the distance. "Let's go tell the Carringtons that Nell's been evicted. I'll explain everything."

16

We walked back to the house. Henry Carrington was waiting for us at the front door, and we followed him to the sitting room, where a fire had been lit, the flames casting long shadows on the walls. Eleanor was sitting on the sofa, and both her face and that of her husband were full of confusion.

"So?" Henry said.

Atticus stayed standing, his hands clasped behind his back as he found the right place to start. "Maeve and Clive Barrett have just been arrested," he said.

Eleanor's mouth fell open. "What?"

"I'm afraid so. Every 'supernatural' event in this house was orchestrated by them. It was staged to make you believe you were being haunted."

"Why would they do that?"

"They were working with Jameson Auster. Their ultimate aim was to scare you out of the house—to sell it at a discount. Auster would like to buy it back. He'd offered to pay them if they could make you leave."

"My God," Henry said. "That's..." He couldn't find the words, shook his head and stared into the fire.

"That's *monstrous*," his wife finished for him.

"It's also criminal," I added.

"They'll be charged?"

"They'll be interviewed," Atticus said, "and, yes, I suspect they will be charged. The police will probably want to take your view on that."

"They need to throw the book at them," Henry said. "They've made our lives miserable for *weeks*."

"You'll get a call from the police in the morning. They'll probably want to come and have a look around. They'll certainly want to see the tunnel."

"Henry showed me," Eleanor said. "Where does it go?"

"The chapel. They were using that as their way to get into and out of the house without being seen."

"I don't understand," she said. "Why would there be a tunnel?"

"I'll explain—and I'll need to show you something else, too."

Atticus led the way to the bedroom where the vase had been smashed earlier that evening. Nothing had been cleared away, and the fragments were still spread across the floor. Atticus stepped over them and went to the fireplace.

"They were in here tonight," Atticus said.

"How, though?" Eleanor said. "They get into the house through the tunnel—I get that—but there are cameras on all the stairs leading up here. We've never seen anything on any of those cameras—not once. How did they get up here without using the stairs?"

"Your house has been hiding some secrets," Atticus said. "The tunnel, for a start, but that's not the only one."

Atticus crouched down and stepped into the inglenook fireplace, running his fingers along the soot-darkened stones. He edged farther back, pressing against the thick oak beam that ran horizontally across the top of the fireplace's recess. His fingers found purchase in a shallow groove, and with a firm push, the beam shifted with a low groan. Dust and soot tumbled down as the wood swung forward on concealed hinges, revealing a narrow cavity in the stonework behind it.

Henry let out a sharp breath. Eleanor's hand went to her mouth.

"What is it?" Henry asked.

"What do you know about priest holes?"

Henry shrugged. "Nothing."

"Watch."

A rusted iron ring was embedded in the stone inside the gap. Atticus grasped it, giving it a firm tug. There was a moment's hesitation, as if the mechanism had long been reluctant to move, then—*click*—the entire side panel of the fireplace shifted. A section of the wall pivoted inward, revealing a dark opening beyond. A wave of cold air rolled out.

They both stared at the opening with mouths agape; I did, too.

"The Auster family were prominent Catholics," Atticus said. "Hallows House was built by Neville Auster in 1560. Elizabeth I issued the Act of Supremacy in 1559, and priest hunters went looking for papists. Being a Catholic was a good way to get yourself arrested or executed—and not pleasantly, either, they were hanging, drawing and quartering in those days. At some point after the house was built, Neville would've drawn up plans to add precautions to keep himself and his family safe."

"Priest holes," I said.

"Exactly—places to hide and ways to escape. One of those precautions was the tunnel, running from the house to the chapel, that would allow them to move back and forth without being seen. It would also give them a way to get out if they needed to. And this"—Atticus pointed into the darkness—"was how the family could get down to the tunnel if there were priest hunters in the house."

Atticus took out his torch, switched it on and shone the beam into the cavity. It was difficult to make out much, but the rungs of a ladder were visible.

Eleanor looked stunned. "It's been here the whole time, and we didn't know."

"That's sort of the point," Atticus said. "They weren't designed to be easily found."

"How did you know it was there, though?"

"I didn't know, not for sure, but I suspected something like it. If we accept that ghosts don't exist and couldn't have caused the events you asked us to investigate—and we must accept that—and then we add the fact that it would have been very difficult to get into the house with all the security measures you installed, then we are left with three possible explanations for what was happening: first, the two of you are responsible, and that doesn't make any sense; second, it's someone with a legitimate reason to be in the house hiding inside until it's dark; or, third, there's a way in that avoids the cameras. Either of the last two possibilities would require a way for someone to move around without being seen.

"I know about priest holes, so I did a little research. I couldn't find anything specific about this particular house, but I did find reference to it in a biography of Nicholas Owen. There's no reason that name would be familiar to you, but he was the most famous builder of priest holes just after the house was built. His biographer believes he was working in Salisbury in the 1590s—there's reference to a property he may have worked on in a letter from a Jesuit priest in 1593. The letter mentions 'a house most cunningly wrought for refuge, with secret chambers devised by the most skilled of craftsmen'. It wasn't named outright, but the description—private chapel, nestled within woodland, a half-day's ride east from Salisbury—matches this estate."

"But knowing there might be secret passages doesn't mean they'd be easy to find," I said.

"Very true. I went about it another way. The fact that the cameras inside the house didn't show anyone moving about made it obvious that whoever was responsible knew where the cameras were and was able to move around in the blind spots. The list of people with that knowledge is limited: the technicians who installed them, but they'd have no motive to conduct a campaign like this against you; the cook, perhaps, but I thought it unlikely that she would've known about *all* of the cameras; your cleaner would know; and so would your housekeeper. We spoke to Maeve, as you know, and she was the one who seemed most invested in Black Nell."

"The story about seeing the body hanging from the bridge?" Eleanor said. "She told you that?"

"She did."

"She told me that, too," Eleanor said.

"I went to her house earlier tonight and waited there. She came out with her husband at half past midnight and drove back to the estate. They parked outside, slipped through a gate in the wall and walked to the chapel. I waited outside—I heard them talking about what they would do and then heard the trapdoor open. I texted Jez to tell him to expect a disturbance and then followed them through the tunnel. They weren't in the cellar when I arrived, but they'd left open the second hidden door. I looked inside and saw the ladder inside the chimney breast. It's over four hundred years old, and it's still robust."

Eleanor had gone pale. "How did Maeve know about it?"

"Her family has worked here for decades. I can't say for sure, but if you asked me to guess, I'd say that Mad Jack discovered it when he lived here and used it and the story of Black Nell to embellish his spiritual retreats."

Eleanor pressed a hand to her forehead. "This is *insane*."

Henry muttered a curse under his breath. "So what now?"

"Maeve and Clive will be charged with trespassing, criminal damage, and harassment at the very least. Possibly more, depending on what the police uncover."

Eleanor looked at Atticus. "And you're sure there's nothing… unnatural going on?"

Atticus smiled. "If there were, I suspect Maeve would have been just as frightened as you."

17

Atticus and I have worked on many cases after Hallows House, but few have had quite as dramatic an unmasking, and none involved a fabricated haunting.

The Carringtons stayed in the house. After everything, I hadn't been sure they would; the ordeal had shaken them, but they were not the type to be scared away. In the months following, they'd taken significant steps to mend their fractured relationship with the village. The old footpath, closed off in the early days of their ownership, had been reopened without fuss or fanfare; a quiet peace offering to those who'd resented their arrival. Their plans for a spa had been scaled down and redesigned, with more sensitivity to the surrounding landscape. Some still grumbled, but most opposition faded. Over time, the hostility towards them dulled, and while they would never be wholly accepted as locals, they were no longer the unwelcome outsiders they'd once been.

Jameson Auster remained in the village, running the pub that he had purchased after selling Hallows House. The bitterness that had coloured his interactions in the early days had given way to something quieter, resignation perhaps. He had written to the Carringtons after everything was exposed, an awkward apology that acknowledged his own role in fanning the resentment against them and for encouraging the Barretts. He denied offering them money in return for forcing the Carringtons out, and it would ultimately be impossible for the police to prove otherwise. Auster said that he had watched, hoping the Carringtons might leave and that he could somehow reclaim the estate. But they had stayed, and he had come to accept that Hallows House was no longer his.

The Carringtons had decided not to push for the Barretts to be charged, and, without their support—and with no real damage done—the police chose not to send the file to the CPS. Atticus managed to get a copy of the police interviews with them both, and I read how Maeve had seen herself as the custodian of the house long before the Carringtons arrived. She had convinced herself she was doing the right thing in trying to drive them away but had underestimated them. She was spared prosecution, but both her and her husband lost their jobs.

One final revelation was still to be delivered. The Carringtons had finally examined the so-called coffin of Black Nell. Forensic analysis of the remains had confirmed what Atticus had suspected all along: there had never been a Nell Kierkegaard. The bones inside the display case were not human, but animal, likely placed there decades ago by Jameson Auster's infamous great-grandfather. The legend had been carefully constructed by Mad Jack, a tall tale spun from fragments of local myths and half-truths, turned into something marketable for guests who wanted a thrill. There was no vengeful spirit, no curse;

just a story that had outlived its creator, given weight by the power of belief and the fear of the unknown.

I visited the village the other day and diverted along the road that led to the house. Money had been spent to renovate it, and a sign on the driveway advertised it as a boutique hotel that would soon be accepting bookings. I pulled over, took out my phone and navigated to the website. It was to be a high-end destination, with prices to match, and had secured the services of a Michelin-starred chef to run the kitchen.

I took in the artistically shot images of the manicured grounds, the elegantly furnished suites, and the candlelit dining room. The Carringtons had leaned into the estate's long history, highlighting its Elizabethan origins and the painstaking restoration that had brought it back to its former grandeur.

Then I saw it: a page titled *The Legend of Black Nell*.

Curious, I tapped the link, half-expecting a sanitisation of the story we'd debunked. Instead, the Carringtons had chosen to embrace the myth in a knowing, almost playful way.

"Hallows House has stood for over four centuries, its walls steeped in history, its halls whispered to be home to more than just its guests. The most enduring legend is that of Black Nell, a spirit said to have wandered these rooms for centuries. While no evidence of her tragic tale has ever been proven, those who stay may find themselves wondering—was it the wind or something else *that moved in the night?"*

Beneath the text was a photograph of the coffin, now encased in glass and displayed in what they called *Nell's Room*, a feature of the new hotel bar. The marketing was clever; enough mystery to draw in those who wanted to believe, but with a knowing wink to those who didn't. And, I thought, it allowed Nell to stay at the house.

Despite everything that had been uncovered, the Carringtons had still decided not to push their luck…

ABOUT MARK DAWSON

Mark Dawson is the author of the John Milton, Beatrix and Isabella Rose and Atticus Priest series. He lives in Salisbury.

For more information:

www.markjdawson.com
mark@markjdawson.com

GET EXCLUSIVE MARK DAWSON MATERIAL